Bone Trail

K-9 Mystery Series, Book 3

Bev Pettersen

Published by Westerhall Books, 2022.

Copyright 2022 Bev Pettersen

Westerhall Books

Editor: Pat Thomas

ISBN: 978-1-987835-28-1

For the exceptional Trisha Doucette and her caring heart

CHAPTER ONE

G unner looked like a healthy dog. Nikki Drake slowed her jog, analyzing his movement as he trotted from tree to tree, sniffing the wooded trail. Now that her German shepherd was no longer glued to her hip, it was easier to check his gait. And be grateful that he had healed from his gunshot wound.

Perhaps he didn't stride out quite as far with his left front leg as he did with his right. But staff at the K9 center had done an excellent job with his rehab. He was walking and running, showing little weakness. Physically at least.

Now it was his aversion to men that caused a problem. He'd always been wary of strangers. Now he was flat-out aggressive. But being shot by a trusted friend tended to do that.

Justin was the only man Gunner allowed close to Nikki. And that was fine, since he was the only man she wanted close. But it would make her PI job difficult when they returned to the city. No one wanted to be around a hostile shepherd. She might have to accept that he would only show his kind nature if he were kept away from other people.

Swallowing her worries, she veered onto the abandoned logging road and picked up the pace. Gunner's ears were pricked and his tail was out, and he looked confident and relaxed as he scouted the overgrown trail ahead.

She skirted a stand of fir trees, leaping over exposed bony roots, following Gunner along their usual route. For the past ten days, she and Justin had run this way every morning. Rarely had they encountered any hikers on this side of the California national forest. The only area close to other people was where the trail opened into a small meadow adjoining the backside of a luxurious horse farm.

That meadow was Gunner's favorite place to stop. He'd struck up a friendship with an inquisitive bay horse named Chico who liked to visit over the fence. It had worked out perfectly as the grassy area was the perfect place to stretch out and do some calisthenics.

She jogged from the woods onto the sparse grass of the clearing, following her eager dog. Strangely the horse paddock adjoining the meadow was empty; Chico was nowhere in sight.

Gunner looked puzzled then disappointed. He wandered along the fence line, marking several posts and lifting his nose to check the breeze gusting from the stable.

Nikki dropped to the grass, keeping a careful eye on her dog, and began her regular series of pushups. Until Justin left, this had also been her favorite spot and the site of several good-natured competitions. Naturally Justin always won but a couple of times she'd nearly beat him in ab crunches. Her fitness level had never been better but without her boyfriend to challenge, the workout wasn't nearly as exciting.

She rolled onto her back, linked her hands behind her head, and admired a hunting eagle soaring over the tree line. His wing span looked huge against the blue sky and it was rather comforting that Gunner was too big to be considered easy prey.

This was definitely an isolated area and Gunner hadn't had a single aggressive incident. Maybe she'd rent the log cabin another week. Unlike Justin, she was her own boss and could choose when to return to investigative work. Besides, this vacation wasn't only for Gunner. The horror of her last case had left her reeling.

They both needed a break and she wanted to give her dog as much time as necessary. And just hope he'd be able to work safely around strangers again. Or more accurately, around men.

She twisted against the grass, checking on Gunner who was wistfully studying the horses grazing in the distance. Yesterday—their first morning without Justin—he'd remained stuck to her side, stressed about being left as Nikki's sole protector. But now his worried brown eyes didn't follow her every move. He looked like a normal companion dog, not a hero who had put his life on the line. Saving her.

Gunner's courage had come at a high cost though. The experts at the K9 center had warned he should be introduced to people slowly. That he was especially unreliable around crowds and men. And sadly that his aggression issues might be permanent.

She tilted her arm, shielding her eyes against the sun, imagining investigative work without her dog. She'd hate being alone. So would he.

He would never understand why he was being left at home. But the behaviorists believed he might never again be safe in public. Admittedly he had grabbed Dr. Martin's arm. But the vet's skin had barely been broken and the man had moved much too close to Nikki. The fact that Gunner hadn't listened to her commands was more disturbing. If he didn't obey in a low-stress situation, she'd never be able to call him off when he was pumped.

If her cases only involved women and children, everything would be fine. With them, Gunner was consistently gentle. He was also good with animals. Even now his tail wagged as he stared at the distant horses. But having a dog who didn't obey was like walking with a stick of dynamite. Someone could be hurt simply for reaching out to shake her hand.

Sighing, she propped herself up to a sitting position, remembering her last case and how the media had crowded around, shoving microphones in her face, jostling to hear more about the pig murders. Gunner wouldn't have accepted that noisy throng. And while it was doubtful she'd ever again be involved in such a sensational case, even her typical investigative work required interaction with people.

Her phone buzzed. She unzipped the pocket of her running shorts and pulled it out, warily checking caller ID. Media furor had settled over the last few months but happily this was a call she'd always accept.

"Good morning, Sonja," she said.

"When are you coming back?" Sonja asked. "It's depressing seeing your office dark. And my latest clients have been totally boring, asking the same old questions about their love lives and if their pets have been reincarnated." She softened her complaint with a melodic laugh. "There are also a slew of dinner specials at Vinny's and it's impossible to get a table without you. Everyone wants to see you and Gunner."

Nikki's mouth tightened and she was glad her friend couldn't see her reaction. It hurt to accept that her beloved dog might never again be able to lie on a restaurant patio. But it would only take one person walking too close...or what Gunner considered too close. And she could never forgive herself if he bit an innocent person.

"We'll probably stay another week," she said lightly. "Justin was called back so it's just Gunner and me now."

"Obviously the city needs its top homicide detective," Sonja said dryly. She and Justin didn't have much in common other than their desire to be polite, for Nikki's sake. "But how are you and Gunner handling being stuck in the wilderness?" Sonja added. "Is he bored without a job to do and someone to intimidate?"

"What do you mean?" Nikki hadn't planned to reveal her concerns—not yet—but her psychic friend had picked up things before and it was never wise to discount anything Sonja said. "Gunner doesn't want to hurt anyone," she added, a little too defensively.

"Of course not," Sonja said. "But that dog needs a job. I can't imagine either of you being happy hiding."

"We're not hiding."

"But you're not seeing anyone either. It's not just media you're trying to avoid."

Nikki leaned forward. It was impossible to keep anything from Sonja. That was one thing both Sonja and Justin did have in common. They were both irritatingly astute.

"Gunner bit someone," Nikki admitted. "At the clinic. It was the day before he was discharged so it couldn't be blamed on pain. Worse, he didn't listen when I tried to call him off. So it's best to keep him away from men for a while. Until I'm sure he can be trusted. They're already talking about removing him from the approved K9 consult list."

"But you mentioned seeing a groom during your morning runs. There wasn't any problem with Gunner then."

"That groom is female."

Sonja was silent for a second. "Okay, well what does Gunner do when you meet male hikers? There must be some of those wandering through the woods."

"No, this section is really isolated. That's why I chose it. And the rare times we meet anyone, I put him on a leash. I can't trust him not to turn aggressive."

"But it's a two-way street. He has to learn to trust your judgment again too."

Nikki grimaced. Yes, she'd been betrayed by a family friend. A man she had trusted with her life. But she didn't like to think it was her poor judgment that had caused Gunner's problems.

"It's my commands he needs to trust," she muttered. "Not me."

"Yes, but Gunner is a highly intelligent dog. His goal is to keep you safe. In his mind, he let someone get close that he shouldn't have. So he's extra protective now, deciding that he knows best. Until you prove yourself to him, he isn't going to change. Cocooning him won't help."

Nikki scrambled to her feet, brushing off a dried leaf along with her frustration. Sometimes Sonja's ideas were so left field, they were hard to absorb. Prove herself to her dog? It was reassuring to think Gunner's aggressiveness was temporary but the notion that he questioned her judgment was ridiculous. And while Sonja had a successful psychic business, she wasn't a dog expert. Not like the psychologists at the K9 center.

"He's a highly trained police dog," Nikki said. "He can't act on his own."

"But he's not a police dog." Sonja's laugh, usually so melodious, was rather grating. "He failed basic training. That's how you got him. And he's already proven that if he doesn't trust his handler, he won't listen."

"I'm not just his handler," Nikki snapped. She kicked a fist-sized stone, sending it rocketing beneath the fence. Gunner raced toward the fence, thinking it was something she wanted retrieved.

"Leave it, Gunner!" she called.

He slid to a stop, the picture of obedience.

"He listens to most things," she added, her eyes on Gunner who remained rooted in place, waiting for her next command. "But that's when we're alone. I'm just afraid what he'll do around strange men."

"He senses your emotions are battered," Sonja said. "He was in rehab during the pig case. But he knows something terrible happened. That it left you affected. Angry."

"You're saying I'm the problem? Not him?"

Sonja didn't answer, her silence heavy.

"Did Justin say something?" Nikki asked. Admittedly, she had lost her temper with a journalist. However, she'd barely touched the man, even after he'd pushed her elderly client and accused the woman's grandson of deserving to be tortured. She thought she'd done well controlling her anger.

"Justin would never say anything," Sonja said. "Not to me. But Gunner reflects your state of mind. Always has, always will. And you're never satisfied unless you're helping someone."

Nikki stared over the crisscross of white paddock fences. She didn't like to think it was her emotions causing Gunner's problems. Maybe staying away from people wasn't the right move. But she *had* been affected by recent events. People had been tortured in that pig barn. Horribly murdered. Even with her psychologist's help, that anger wasn't easy to shake off.

"I've got to go," she murmured, shoving away the bloody images. "We've got three more miles to run, and it doesn't look like Gunner's horse friend is here. Give Stormy a pat for us."

"Wait," Sonja said. "So that means you won't see a single person today? That can't be good, for either of you."

"It's fine. Besides, we'll see Ana and the horse tomorrow. They're always here."

"Obviously that's not true," Sonja said. "Because she's not there today. How can you and Gunner learn to be comfortable with people again if you don't see anyone?

"Why don't you come back and stay at my place?" she went on. "Gunner can hang out with your pony and all the other critters. You can leave trails for him to follow, give him a job to do. There's lots of space and the media will never find you."

Nikki tilted her head. Sonja had a small acreage that was home to all types of rescue animals, including Stormy, Nikki's retired pony. Gunner loved the place and it was where he'd honed his tracking skills. It was also much closer to the city. And to Justin.

"You'll be able to see Justin too," Sonja added, as if reading her mind. "And I promise not to make either of you sit for any tea leaf readings."

Nikki gave a rusty laugh followed by a wave of optimism. Sonja's place was commutable to the city but also very private. It would be a good way to ease Gunner back into society, before he had to face hordes of people.

He still sat by the fence, head cocked, staring wistfully toward the barns. An oval training track stretched toward the south but there was no sign of any activity. Only horses grazing in groups of two and three. But Chico, the compact bay that was usually in this remote paddock, was nowhere in sight. Nor was Ana, the horse's groom.

At Sonja's place, Gunner would be able to get close to the animals. Nikki could control his activity and make him feel as if he had a job. It was the better choice.

"We'd love to come to your place, thanks," she said gratefully. "We'll pack up and be there before dark."

She slipped the phone back in her pocket, taking one last glance around for Ana. It was odd the woman wasn't here. She always brought Chico for grass after his morning gallop and was comfortable with large dogs. She and her horse had become part of Gunner's routine.

Yesterday Ana even shared a piece of carrot with Gunner. He'd checked with Nikki first, waiting for the signal that it was okay. And it had been reassuring to see him take the treat from Ana's hand, so gently and with a total lack of suspicion. The K9 therapists would have been pleased.

"Let's go, fellow," she said, turning toward the wooded trail. "We can't wait around for a horse. Besides, you'll see Stormy tonight."

And he'd be able to play with the pony. Here, Gunner had to stay on the other side of the fence. Ana had looked aghast when Nikki asked if he could go in Chico's paddock.

"No, no, no!" she'd said. "You shouldn't even be this close. The owner wouldn't like it." Ana had gestured at one of the several No Trespassing signs before calming her voice. "Besides, Chico is a Thoroughbred. High spirited and sensitive. If he runs out of control, he could get hurt. And I'm getting him ready for an important race."

Chico didn't seem especially sensitive, at least not when Gunner was around. In fact, the two animals had played along the fence line, and even Ana had smiled at their camaraderie. It was unfortunate Ana wasn't around today. It would have been nice to say goodbye. Clearly though, she wasn't coming.

Nikki gave one last look around then headed for the brush at the back of the clearing. Gunner loped past her, taking up his position scouting the trail ahead. But they'd barely passed the far corner of the paddock before he jerked to a stop.

"What's wrong?" she asked, peering in the direction of his pricked ears.

He whined, nostrils flaring. Obviously he wanted to check out a tantalizing scent, no doubt some sort of wild animal. It wouldn't hurt to let him take a quick detour. No one was around and it would compensate for his lack of social time with Chico. Gunner would be much happier if he thought he'd completed a job.

She waved her arm and he shot forward. A startled pheasant rose from the grass, its wings thumping in alarm, but Gunner wasn't distracted and stayed on the scent. She watched him closely. Didn't want him out of sight or anywhere near the distant buildings.

When he jumped over the paddock fence, she opened her mouth to call him back. But there was no need. Just beyond the gate, he stopped and sat, signifying a find. He looked back, awaiting her command.

"Good dog," she said. "Bring it."

He shoved his nose into the grass and triumphantly headed back, something pale gripped between his jaws. Possibly the remains of an unfortunate rabbit, its killer spooked by their appearance.

Gunner leaped back over the fence and deposited his find at her feet, clearly anticipating praise. But she didn't give her usual encouragement. Could only stare.

For this was no wild animal.

It was an arm: pinkish white flesh pitted with dirt and severed below the elbow. Stubs marked the spot of each missing finger. It wasn't bloody and carried a faint whiff of rot.

She jerked away, the sound of her heartbeat thrashing in her ears. This isn't like the pig farm, she told herself. It's not like that. But she had to pull in several fortifying breaths before she could calm her thumping heart. Then, steadying herself against Gunner's back, she reached for her phone.

CHAPTER TWO

Nikki studied the seven men gathered around two county police vehicles. The police had met her in the back parking lot of the horse stable within thirty minutes of her phone call. So far, not much was happening.

The bald policeman kept bobbing his head while a blond man in a black Armani style jacket gestured. Other than the three uniformed cops, it was impossible to tell who was with the stable and who represented law enforcement. Not one of them looked, or acted, like a detective. The distance was too far to hear actual words but they were obviously acquainted, judging by all the congenial nods.

The bald cop had been much more officious with her. In fact, he'd barely spoken after swooping up in his police car, instructing that she wait by the hay shed so that her dog wouldn't scare the horses. He'd totally misinterpreted why she'd been keeping such a tight hold of Gunner's leash. And why she'd been so agreeable about waiting far away from the men.

"Good boy," she said, relieved Gunner was acting so calm. He watched the group of men with suspicious eyes but remained seated by her side, the picture of obedience.

There had been one tense moment when she'd first approached the buildings. They'd entered along the side of a rear lane, cutting through a row of privacy trees and past an imposing horse monument flanked by several headstones. Seconds after she'd noted a camouflaged security camera, a surprised guard had charged out.

He'd been aggressive, clearly not welcoming foot traffic, and Gunner had taken exception to his forceful approach. But after she'd explained her gruesome find—and that police had instructed her to meet them at the stable—the guard had nodded and waved her through. And Gunner had seemed reassured the man wasn't a threat.

She scratched the base of his left ear, wondering how long they'd have to hang around. They might want Gunner's help in the search. In her call to the police, she'd provided the location where he'd found the severed arm. But at this point it was impossible to guess the actual crime area.

Unfortunately, hikers occasionally went missing in state parks, either through misadventure or murder. It didn't appear that wildlife had been gnawing at the arm so perhaps the rest of the body was nearby. She suppressed a little shiver. Gunner wasn't ready to go back to work yet. Neither was she.

Her last case was too fresh in her mind. And no matter how hard she tried to block it, the sight of that arm left her picturing greedy pigs rooting through human remains. Even the sweet smell of alfalfa from the nearby hay shed couldn't soften the remembered stink of blood and bone. Frankly, she just wanted to pack up and drive to Sonja's, where she could sit on her friend's sagging porch, share a bottle of wine and admire the calming sunset.

Besides, the bald cop hadn't been interested in talking. Had brushed her off when she tried to give her name and Gunner's credentials. At least they'd retrieved the arm without difficulty. It had been bagged and placed in a county cruiser; the sheriff's emblem was emblazoned on the vehicle door. Beyond that she couldn't see much police activity.

She dragged her hand over the back of Gunner's neck. It had been over fifty minutes since the police had spoken to her, and it was getting tedious watching the men chat. It was also turning hot. The sun had climbed and the side of the hay shed no longer offered any shade. Gunner's tongue was hanging out, his pants much louder.

His tail abruptly thumped the ground, his friendly greeting rather surprising. He wasn't a dog who welcomed strangers. He was looking away from the men though, toward the barns. A worker was approaching. It took her a moment to realize that it was Ana. And she was carrying a bucket.

"For Gunner," the woman said, her voice so low it was almost inaudible.

"Thank you." Nikki smiled at Ana, happy to see her.

But Ana didn't linger. Her gaze skittered toward the police cars and she set the bucket down so fast that water sloshed over the side. Then she turned and hurried away, her head tucked, tortoise-like, into her shoulders.

Clearly she was worried about the police presence. Maybe she worked illegally. Judging by the number of barns, the stable required a large number of staff. It would be a good job for someone who needed accommodation yet preferred to remain far away from official eyes.

Ana certainly talked and moved differently. By the paddock she strode with authoritative grace, every bit as confident as her horse. Several times she had even discussed breeding lines with Justin, arguing that South American Thoroughbreds were some of the hardiest in the world.

But today that natural assurance had disappeared, her voice and body shrunken. If she hadn't bolted so quickly, Nikki would have reassured her that the current police presence wasn't related to undocumented workers.

Gunner lapped noisily at the water then lifted his dripping muzzle, watching as Ana scurried toward a long row of rectangular barns.

It was his worried whine that prompted Nikki to scramble to her feet. She should soothe Ana's fears. It would also be nice to have the chance to say goodbye. Ana and her horse had been the highlight of Gunner's days here, and the interaction had helped with his socialization.

Besides, she wasn't going to make Gunner wait in this heat any longer, especially since the police were standing around, chatting like members of an old boys' club.

"Heel, Gunner," she said, scooping up the bucket and following Ana.

She steeled herself for a shout. But even though she was moving away from the police, nobody called for her to stop. The only sounds were the rumble of voices and the occasional guffaw. Certainly no one seemed in a hurry to search for more body parts.

Shaking her head, she rounded the side of the hay shed, trailing Ana's retreating figure. A stocky man with a buzz cut and a radio clipped to his belt stepped from an attendant's booth.

Nikki wasn't dressed for the stable, but investigative work had taught her how to fake it. Acting confident was essential. The bucket was also a great prop. She raised a hand and waved, pretending to acknowledge someone beyond the guard. Gunner did his part too, walking quietly on the leash and ignoring the man.

The guard hesitated then stepped back into the booth, leaving her free to enter the barn area.

Ana was about thirty feet ahead and moving fast. She hurried past two buildings then scooted into the yawning entrance of barn three. Nikki quickened her stride, reassured by Gunner's good behavior. He seemed tolerant with the men here as long as they didn't enter her personal space.

They stepped through the doorway of the barn. But the aisle was empty of everything except a blue wheelbarrow shoved against the wall.

Ana must have exited out the end door, maybe taking a short cut to the dorms set to the east of the property. And there would be way too much commotion there for Gunner. Crowds were the last thing he needed.

At least the barn was more comfortable than sitting outside. Whirring fans kept it refreshingly cool. As long as she had a bucket in her hand, she could probably linger in the barn. She'd rather admire the beautiful Thoroughbreds than stare at the chatting men.

It was definitely a luxurious facility, geared for comfort as well as appearance. The aisle was spotless with thick rubber mats cushioning her steps. Brass hooks hung beside the stall doors along with polished nameplates that proclaimed each horse's name along with their sire and dam. She knew from Justin's passion for racehorses the bloodlines that were most valued, and many of the stud names were familiar.

Several horses looked at Gunner, then raised their heads and gave suspicious snorts. Judging by their reaction they weren't accustomed to dogs so perhaps the bucket wouldn't be enough of a prop to stay in the barn for long.

No one could fault Gunner's behavior though. He looked straight ahead, ignoring the snorting horses and maintaining his dignified walk. She gave his head an approving pat. This was excellent progress. He'd been exposed to several situations today, including the first guard whose body language had been less than friendly. And he'd remained obedient, following every command.

And then the leash tightened as Gunner jerked to a stop. She gave a little tug but he refused to move. Instead, he sat on his haunches, staring stubbornly at the third stall from the end. The brass sign by the stall said CHICO'S KID (CH).

A familiar brown horse stuck his head over the door. Unlike the other horses, Chico wasn't one bit fearful or haughty. Pressing his chest against the door, he stretched his neck until his nose met Gunner's. They greeted each other like old friends.

Ana's head popped up from behind the stall door. "Don't feed him," she said.

"Of course not," Nikki said, impressed at how protective Ana always was of the horse. And now it was obvious why Ana hadn't been visible in the aisle. She had stepped into Chico's stall and latched the door from the outside.

"I just wanted to thank you for the water," Nikki added. "And to say goodbye. We're leaving today so won't be coming by the paddock again. I really appreciate how good you were with Gunner."

Ana gave a distracted nod, turning and peering toward the wide end door. The skin over her cheekbones was unusually drawn and dark circles shadowed her eyes. She was definitely spooked.

"The police are here about something Gunner found," Nikki said gently. "It's nothing to do with the staff."

Ana's head swung around, her dark eyes locked on Nikki's face. "What did Gunner find?"

Nikki hesitated. Much of her job depended on getting along with authorities and she didn't know what details police would reveal. A camper might already have been reported missing. It would be horrible for a family to prematurely hear that human remains had been discovered. And Justin had often remarked how the strategic release of information could make the difference in a murder conviction.

"It was just something by the wilderness park," Nikki said. "This stable was the closest point for vehicle access. So the police asked me to meet them here."

But the concern on Ana's face didn't change. If anything she turned even paler. Maybe Nikki's assumption of illegal workers was off base, and something else was bothering Ana. Maybe Chico was sick. Her devotion to the horse was obvious. And Chico hadn't been turned out in his usual paddock today.

Nikki glanced over the stall door, scanning Chico's legs. He'd greeted Gunner with his usual enthusiasm but maybe he'd suffered an injury in his morning workout.

There didn't seem to be anything wrong though. Thick yellow straw reached almost to his knees but it was apparent his legs weren't bandaged. He was bright and happy and seemed to be eating and drinking. A water bucket was clipped to the wall alongside a red hay net. Everything in the stall looked typical—except for a thin army blanket neatly folded in the corner.

Along with the blanket was a water bottle, a paperback and what looked like a nylon travel bag, although most of the bag was tucked in the straw. Ana was obviously sleeping here which was odd considering the worker dorms on site. It seemed unlikely that someone who'd worked here so long wouldn't rate a room.

"Do you want to sleep here?" Nikki asked.

"Lately." Ana's pinched gaze shot back down the aisle. "Just until Chico's race tomorrow. Hopefully after that we can move back to Chile."

"Is that what the CH on his nameplate means? Chico is from Chile too?"

"Yes." Ana's voice strengthened with pride. Now she seemed more like the woman Nikki and Justin had met in the clearing. "He was born and bred there. His dam was Chilean Horse of the Year. I've been his groom since he was weaned. You can pat him if you want. He's very gentle, unlike some stallions."

Nikki reached out and scratched Chico's muscled neck. This was the closest she'd been to him. Always before they'd been separated by the paddock fence.

Chico had an endearing splash of white on his forehead along with kind and intelligent eyes. He and Gunner had clearly developed a rapport. For two weeks, she'd watched them play up and down the fence line. At first she'd worried that an energetic Thoroughbred might strike out with a foreleg. But Chico seemed to understand his strength, even in play. And now Gunner pressed against the stall door, so close Chico could sniff his back, completely trusting that the horse wouldn't nip.

She wasn't quite so trusting. Chico had been fine outdoors but he might be protective of his stall. Several of Justin's stallions were unpredictable. Prone to sudden and painful bites.

"Chico won't hurt your dog," Ana said. "And I already know Gunner won't hurt Chico. They are alike. Strong minded but total gentlemen."

Nikki gave an agreeable nod. However, she wished it were that simple. If Gunner was so gentle, she could head back to her office right now. Take on a new case and get back to work, with her dog by her side. There'd also be no worries about being removed from the K9 consult list. Ana's concern about Chico seemed complicated too. Perhaps it was the horse's behavior that necessitated her sleeping in his stall.

"Does Chico act up when you're not around? Is that why you warned me not to feed him?"

"No," Ana said. "He's very well behaved. I just don't want anyone feeding him but me."

"Are there many visitors to the stable?"

"Not anymore. But horses have a fragile digestive system so I have to be careful. Especially this week."

"What's different about this week?"

"You should go," Ana said, abruptly jamming her hands in her pockets. "I'm surprised you got past the guard. It isn't good to draw attention to Chico."

"Why not?" Clearly Ana didn't like a lot of questions but curiosity came with Nikki's profession. And the woman's discomfort was troubling.

Authoritative voices sounded just beyond the end door.

"Go," Ana whispered, her eyes widening as she dropped out of sight behind the stall door.

Nikki quickly edged away from Chico's stall, guiding Gunner into the middle of the aisle, just as two men swept through the far entrance. She couldn't see their faces, only their silhouettes. However, as they moved closer she recognized the bald cop who'd told her to wait by the hay shed. He was accompanied by the blond man in the designer jacket.

"Easy," she said, touching Gunner's head in warning. He didn't like swaggering men. But it would be a dark mark on his record if he bit a cop. And the fact that Ana was hiding showed that her experience with the police hadn't been positive. Nikki certainly wasn't impressed with the local force.

She edged further down the aisle, hoping to draw the cop's attention away from Chico's stall. He wouldn't spot Ana unless he leaned over the door and checked the corner of the stall.

"I told you to wait outside," the cop said.

"Just looking for a tap so I could give my dog some water," she said, waving the bucket. "He was thirsty after such a long wait."

The cop glanced at the blond man beside him as though checking his reaction. Then he whipped out his notebook. "I need your name," he said, scowling as if it were her fault he hadn't recorded it earlier.

"Nikki Drake," she said, her voice equally clipped. She didn't add that she was a licensed private investigator and that Gunner might be able to help find the remains. So far, the police hadn't inspired much confidence and the fact that Ana had hidden behind the stall door wasn't reassuring.

"I'm David Durant," the blond man said, unsmiling. "The owner of this race stable. Thank you for calling the police."

He didn't sound grateful. And he didn't dress like a hands-on horseman. His Armani jacket and ostentatious belt buckle were way over the top. The belt was even studded with diamonds which she figured were probably real; the man reeked of money and entitlement.

"Looks like you were out for a little run," Durant added, his condescending gaze sweeping over her, from the top of her thick ponytail down to her well-worn running shoes.

"Yes."

"Was anyone else with you?"

"No." She looked at the cop, wondering why he was letting a civilian take over the interview. If this even was an interview. The cop had already put away his notebook.

"So you were the only person to see this bone?" Durant asked.

"That's right." She refrained from mentioning that she'd taken several pictures.

"You seem to have lost your way." Durant's voice sharpened. "Can you explain to us why you were jogging on private property?"

What a bully, she thought, tightening her grip on Gunner's leash. He'd established she was alone and assumed he could intimidate. Little wonder Ana wanted to stay out of sight.

"I was following the trail at the east end," she said. "The one that cuts through the clearing. That's state property, at least according to my map."

Durant's mouth tightened. Obviously he wanted people to believe he owned a portion of the park. He stared for a moment as if trying to figure her out.

"That's an odd area to be jogging," he said. "Rough trails and lots of wildlife. It's unsafe, especially for a woman."

"But it's safe for men?"

"Everyone is warned to stay away," Durant snapped. "We don't even use that end paddock. It's too remote and I just don't want anyone to get hurt."

Too late for that, she thought. Because someone was missing an arm. And Ana had used that paddock for the past two weeks so Durant's statement was a blatant lie. Gunner whined, sensing her agitation, and she placed a calming hand on his head.

Durant saw her gesture and his thin lips curved. But his smile contained no warmth. "You also need to be warned," he said, "that my men have orders to deal with any animal—wild or domestic—that harasses my horses."

No doubt, this man had his own definition of harass, and the policeman beside Durant gave little comfort. In fact, the gun on the cop's hip suddenly seemed threatening. Didn't matter though. She was leaving. Police could bring in a cadaver dog to find the rest of the body. Hopefully their murder investigation would wipe away some of Durant's arrogance.

She hid her aversion with a stiff smile. "Of course," she murmured. "It's natural to worry about your horses. But my dog is good with animals."

"So you claim," Durant said. "But I suggest you take a different route the next time you go for your little jog. It would be much safer. For both you and your dog."

He edged closer, carrying the smoky scent of expensive cologne, using his height to intimidate. But he was looking past her, his expression calculating, and she realized he was trying to provoke Gunner.

Her blood chilled. She stooped, quickly wrapping both hands around Gunner's collar. His hackles were up but at least he wasn't growling. Not yet.

"Yes, a different route would be much safer," Durant went on, his malicious gaze still on Gunner. "Especially with all the hunters who will be congregating."

"Hunters?"

"That's right." The cop finally spoke up. "We need to find that cougar. Mr. Durant has agreed to organize the hunt."

"You think that arm was the result of a cougar attack?" she asked, unable to hide her incredulity.

"Not an arm," Durant snapped. "The bone is from a horse. But a layperson can't be expected to know the difference."

"But I saw it. It's a human arm, cleanly cut."

Durant crossed his arms and looked at the cop, at if relaying a message.

"So you have experience with skeletons?" the cop asked. "Human parts?"

"Of course not," she said, easing Gunner further away from the men. "Probably it was a cougar attack. I only took a quick look. It was very upsetting." She let her voice trail off, even adding a theatrical shiver for good measure.

"That's natural," the cop said. "Any civilian would be upset, seeing what they thought was a human arm."

But Durant wasn't as easy to fool. He was still studying Gunner, his eyes narrowed to slits, as if calculating the best way to provoke. And they were on his property—surrounded by expensive horses—where it seemed this man's word was law. It was definitely time to leave.

She forced a smile. "Okay, well that's great you're looking after it. Good luck with the hunt."

She tugged Gunner's leash, urging him toward the end door, away from Durant and his sidekick cop. But as she walked down the aisle, she felt a following malevolence and the hair rose on the back of her neck.

"Wait," Durant ordered.

Smoothing the dismay from her face, she stopped and turned.

"You're alone," he said. "Obviously far from your car. I'll have someone drive you back. Are you staying in one of the park rentals?"

"That's not necessary," she said. "I can jog back. Find my friends along the way."

"But I insist. A large section of my land adjoins the park. And it would be a tragedy if you, or your dog, were mistaken for that cougar."

Her palms felt annoyingly sticky against the leather leash. She wasn't sure if Durant's threats were real, but his tone was mocking and it was obvious he took a sadistic delight in scaring women. Especially those he considered weak.

She faked a show of enthusiasm. "Okay, thanks. A lift home would be great."

But there was no way she was letting that man know the location of her cabin. It didn't feel wise to step into his vehicle either.

Once outside the barn, she'd turn in the other direction. Get off the property and then decide what to do about the arm. Justin always gave clinical advice. He would steady her. Keep her from turning this personal.

Waving, she turned back toward the door, working hard to keep her steps slow and untroubled. At least Gunner's hackles had lowered. Ten more feet and they'd be out of Durant's sight.

But behind her, the cop was talking on his radio, calling for an escort. And her heart sank.

Moments later, two uniformed policemen appeared in the doorway. One of them gave a brief nod and gestured to the right, directing her to walk past the security booth and around the hay shed. They remained a few steps behind, moving stiffly, and keeping a wary distance from Gunner. She made an attempt at conversation but they ignored it, flanking her as if she was a trespasser, driving home her suspicion that Durant was in control of the authorities.

They approached the rear parking lot. The three men she'd assumed to be plainclothes police were probably Durant employees. They slouched against a dark Cadillac Escalade, as big and powerful as the vehicle. Sunglasses hid their eyes, but one man had his cell phone pressed to his ear, his head turned toward her, as if gathering final instructions.

Probably Durant merely wanted to scare her. Make her forget about the arm Gunner had discovered. But sweat beaded on her forehead. And she'd learned not to ignore her instincts.

"I understand one of you kind gentlemen is going to drive me home," she called brightly. "I just need to use the bathroom first. My bladder is bursting."

She veered in the direction of the worker dorms and kept walking. She had no idea where a bathroom was but once around the side of the hay barn, she whispered, "Let's go, Gunner."

They bolted toward the trees.

It took less than a minute to sprint across the open paddock and scale the railed fence, but it felt like an eternity. Her shoulder blades itched the entire time as if expecting a bullet in the back. She told herself she was imagining trouble. But when she slipped into the sheltering trees, her heart was still pounding and it wasn't from the short run.

She slipped around the perimeter of the woods to the hilly west side. Then dropped to the ground behind a pine tree and studied the stable. Ana hadn't re-emerged and no workers were visible. Clearly they had the good sense to know when to disappear.

She spotted Durant and the bald cop standing by the vehicles, surrounded by an attentive group of men.

Durant gestured. A lean man jogged across the paddock toward the trees where she'd originally entered. He vaulted the fence and his jacket swung open, revealing a shoulder holster. Then he vanished into the trees.

She kept a cautious eye behind her. However after ten minutes the man re-appeared in almost the same spot. He crossed back across the field, carefully weaving around a skittish bunch of horses.

He spoke for a moment and Durant jabbed his thumb. The bald cop nodded and one of the uniformed police removed a white bag from the police cruiser and deposited it in the Escalade. Obviously the police didn't intend to investigate. There was more discussion, even the bark of laughter. No one seemed interested in organizing a cougar hunt.

She pulled out her phone and scrolled over the pictures she'd taken of the arm. Then she forwarded the photos to one of the few people she knew who genuinely understood wildlife. Jack Tanner was only a teen but very blunt and always keen to give his opinion. And he hunted to put food on the table. Hopefully he was somewhere with cell coverage.

"Cougar attack?" she texted beneath the images.

Jack's answer came back almost immediately. *Only if it's a cougar that knows how to operate a buzz saw.*

She leaned back against the smooth bark of the tree, staring at his message. So she was correct: The cuts had been human inflicted. Durant and the cops were full of shit. And that prompted the question as to why they felt the need for a cover-up. And also confirmed that she'd been wise to disappear.

She peeked around the tree, checking on the activity. A quick head count confirmed that all the men were still clustered around Durant. She blew out a breath, relieved she wouldn't have to worry about anyone creeping through the trees. It looked like the police were leaving. There were some friendly handshakes. Then the bald cop squeezed into his cruiser and the other two cops drove off in the second marked car.

Durant wasn't finished though. He gestured again, first toward the spot where she'd disappeared and then toward the clearing. Two of his men jumped into the Escalade and sped down a gravel road, throwing up agitated plumes of dust.

They were probably sent to check the hiking trails. Or park rentals. That would take hours. If she left now she'd have enough time to run back, grab her belongings and head to Sonja's. She'd be long gone before they could pinpoint her cabin. Justin would know the best way to follow up.

But the knowledge that Durant was still searching left her conflicted. Maybe he only wanted to make another threat. Make sure she'd accepted it was a horse bone. Obviously though, a crime had been committed. And that made it difficult to walk away.

"Let's watch a bit longer," she murmured, reaching over and brushing some pine needles off Gunner's back. "I'll leave a message with Justin. Let him know what's happening."

She pressed speed dial, surprised when he answered after the first ring.

"I thought you'd be in court," she said. "How's it going?"

"Short recess. I'm up next. Did you and Gunner finish your run?"

"Not yet. We're still by that horse property. Gunner found something odd."

"Oh, what?" His voice drifted. "Give me a minute," she heard him say to someone. Voices sounded. She recognized the prosecutor's voice. This case was a high profile homicide but conviction hinged on whether the judge ruled that the search had been legal. Justin's testimony would be crucial. She never would have called if she thought he'd pick up his phone. Didn't like to interrupt.

"I'll send a text," she said quickly. "Good luck in there."

"All right. Talk to you tonight."

She cut the connection, picturing Justin in a court setting. He was a consummate professional, smart, articulate and honest. The prosecution didn't have to worry about him bending the rules. And his good looks were an advantage, especially with female members of the jury.

Justin was always the voice of reason. But she didn't want to wait until tonight. She thought for a moment then forwarded the pictures to another contact. Not actually her friend but Justin's: a coroner he'd once dated who was always keen to help. This woman would answer quickly, especially if Nikki worded the request to make it sound as if it came from Justin.

She pressed send. Then stretched out and waited for a reply. Gunner lay beside her, his head resting on his paws. She closed her eyes, confident he would alert her to anyone's approach.

The chirping birds were soothing and she even dozed for a bit. The ping of an incoming text jerked her awake.

She peered at the coroner's message: *Striated marks indicate a saw-toothed blade. Flesh is discolored and pitted, possibly from burial with lye. Likely the forearm is from an adult male cadaver with fingers removed to reduce chance of identification.*

She scanned the message again, now totally alert. So the bone was human. And not the result of a wildlife attack. That meant someone had committed murder and it was likely Durant was involved. But why dig up an arm and leave it where there was a chance it could be discovered? It hadn't even been concealed on Durant's vast property. Gunner had pulled it from the grass by the paddock gate.

She rubbed her forehead. Obviously someone was supposed to find it. Not her though. Durant had been surprised that park visitors even used that trail. The only other person to frequent the clearing was Ana.

It was unfortunate they hadn't had a chance to talk longer. But Durant and the bald cop had shown up almost as soon as Nikki entered the barn, even though they'd left her twiddling her thumbs beside the hay shed for more than an hour. Clearly they hadn't wanted her speaking to staff.

"I think we'll hang around on the ridge a bit longer," she said. "Look for another chance to talk to Ana."

Gunner thumped his tail, keeping up his end of the conversation. He looked eager, seeming to sense their boring day finally had some purpose.

She hoped she didn't regret not bringing his bullet-proof vest.

CHAPTER THREE

Nikki brushed an ant off her running shoe, her gaze shooting back to the property below. After several hours of surveillance, it was clear she wasn't likely to find another chance to talk to Ana. It was also clear the three remaining men were not cops but Durant's private security. The police and the man in the guardhouse used radios to communicate; these private guards used cell phones.

Now the rear parking lot was empty. A guard had accompanied Durant into the opulent house. The other two had split up. One was posted outside barn three. The other strode across the paddocks and disappeared into the state property beyond the clearing. He hadn't emerged.

It was disturbing that a man with a gun had been posted on the trail that she followed to go home. Even more alarming was that she didn't know his location, or his intent. It was doubtful he'd circle around to the south, and Gunner would warn her of his approach, but that didn't stop her uneasiness. It meant she'd have to bushwhack to return to the cabin. Not a big deal but it would definitely take more time and effort. She certainly had some interesting information to pass on to Justin.

"Seen enough?" she asked Gunner. "Ready to go home?"

He just looked at her then laid his big head back on his paws, his eyes fixed on Chico's barn.

She trailed an amused hand over his neck. Gunner knew the word "home" and he clearly didn't want to leave. But letting a dog choose their activities wasn't practical, and she needed to pack up before any unwelcome visitors arrived at the cabin. However, was Durant really looking for her? The Escalade had certainly headed somewhere in a hurry and his private guard was watching the game trail. But that might not be related to her. She also had no idea what the police were doing or how much power Durant had over the local sheriff.

She pulled her phone out again, checking the internet, trying to dig up more information about David Durant. But she had no special access to information and all she'd succeeded in doing was to lower her battery charge.

The investigator who'd mentored her had stressed that inside sources could be the difference between career success and failure, and he'd been correct. She was constantly trying to build up her own contacts and not have to rely on Justin. However, the people she knew were unlikely to answer quickly. Extracting information from them was like pulling teeth. Her fledgling business simply hadn't done enough to cultivate favors from the proper people.

Then she thought of the cop she'd met during the pig case. Sgt. Aaron Smith, aka Smitty, had publicly credited her with saving his life. He'd said he owed her. Time to find out if he meant it.

She texted him, keeping her request simple. *Need info on a David Durant, Thoroughbred horse owner, owner of large southern California race stable. Appreciate anything you can find.*

She stretched out beside Gunner, her arm draped over his shoulders, and tried to relax. Surveillance was typically boring and one of the hardest things for her to learn had been how to wait. Gunner had proven better at it than her.

The sun was lowering in the western sky when her phone pinged with Smitty's reply: *David Durant, philanthropist, animal lover and racehorse enthusiast. Donated twenty million dollars to local hospital following death of his wife two years ago. Lauded for generous profit sharing and creative employee packages with goal of assisting immigrants.*

She blinked at the screen, needing to read the message twice. She'd pegged Durant all wrong. He didn't sound like an abusive employer and probably wasn't involved in any murder. She'd let her dislike for the man push her imagination into overdrive. Perhaps he had been sincere about driving her home. Nothing explained the severed arm or the lame cougar theory but maybe Ana was sleeping in Chico's stall out of choice. And had hidden because of an innate fear of authority.

But moments later a second message from Smitty filled her screen. *David Durant Jr. assumed control of the racing operation following his father's death fourteen months ago. Management changes have resulted in high staff turnover and cancellation of work permits. Two lawsuits were filed by employees claiming they'd been cheated out of a share in the horses' winnings but charges were withdrawn.*

Ah, now this additional information fit with her suspicions. She saw Smitty was typing another message and waited with bated breath.

A bomb threat was called in last month but nothing was found on the Durant property. Local sheriff reported false alarm. That's all I got.

And that was enough, she thought, texting her heartfelt thanks. Maybe Durant Jr. didn't support his father's compensation plan and wanted employees to quit. Forcing them to sleep in stalls along with other intimidation tactics would send employees scurrying. Perhaps Ana was on his list.

She plucked out a twig caught in Gunner's hair, trying to decide if she should head out. It would be dark in an hour. Her stomach was growling and she could almost taste the wine waiting at Sonja's. Justin would be finished with his court testimony tomorrow. She could wait and ask his opinion. He'd know the best approach.

The property below looked totally serene. Earlier, stable hands had hurried back and forth between the barns and paddocks, returning horses to their stalls, but now all was quiet. Someone in the dorms was frying supper and the smell of chicken and onions drifted on the breeze.

Her stomach gave another rumble of protest. It would be easy to walk away and assume that, for now, everything was okay. Workers and horses seemed settled for the evening. No one moved, not even around the imposing house.

When she was back in her office, she'd do some digging. A human arm couldn't be ignored. But for now there seemed to be no urgency.

She rose to her feet, deciding it would still be wise to avoid her usual trail. It would take more time but she could pack up quickly and check out online. She'd drive to Sonja's and finish out her vacation. Start exposing Gunner to a few more people, slowly, one at a time. Give him the best chance for success.

His low whine jerked her attention back to the barns. She followed Gunner's gaze but didn't see anything exciting. Then movement flashed. A man ran around the hay shed, his head on a swivel, as if trying to pinpoint her location.

She pressed back against the tree but quickly realized he wasn't looking for her. His head was down, worrying more about watchers around the barns rather than someone on the ridge.

He was dressed similarly to the other workers: loose jeans, T-shirt, and he was small enough to be an exercise rider. But he moved differently, more furtive. And he wasn't leading a horse. Instead, he cradled something shiny in his hands.

She leaned forward, her adrenaline spiking. Another bomb threat? But this time for real?

The man looked suspicious, darting looks and sneaking around buildings. He was definitely handling the package gingerly. Probably Durant had good reason to employ so many guards. No doubt he'd alienated many employees. She'd disliked him within minutes of their meeting.

Still, she couldn't stand back and watch someone blow up a barn filled with helpless horses. Hopefully the hay shed was the target. Nothing was in there but alfalfa hay and a couple of tractors.

She watched, scarcely daring to breathe. *Please stop at the hay shed.* But the wiry man crept past the shed, the package cradled in front of him. He slipped behind barn one, barn two and slowed at the rear of barn three.

Chico's barn. And Ana was sleeping there. A guard was posted at the front but he might not spot the man. And the attendant in the guardhouse faced the parking lot, not anticipating danger from within.

Groaning, she pushed away from the tree, knowing she couldn't stand by and watch.

Gunner's tail wagged, surprising her with the way it thumped the ground. He always sensed danger before her. Had even received some bomb training at the K9 center. Yet he was wagging his tail, his tongue lolling in a dog smile. Not one bit agitated.

She peered back toward the barn. The man had stopped twenty feet from the end door and was now pressed against the outer wall, directly below a stall window.

A familiar face flashed in the opening—Ana. She leaned through the window, stretching out her arm.

Nikki softened as comprehension hit. It wasn't a bomb, only a plate covered with aluminum foil. She was imagining danger when there wasn't any. Sure, the man had been acting suspiciously but he was only delivering Ana's supper. There was nothing going on here; it was time to leave.

But seconds later, Durant's guard swooped around the corner. He grabbed the man's arm, knocking the plate to the ground. The action was so swift, so brutal, that the little man yelped, Ana screamed and Gunner growled.

CHAPTER FOUR

Nikki grabbed Gunner's collar, straining to see. Ana's face had vanished below the window but the little man cowered in terror, unable to run. The guard held him by the arm and with his other hand pulled out a cell phone. The burly guard didn't talk long, but Nikki saw him nod, as if accepting directions.

The guard replaced his phone and pressed the man against the wall. Then he pulled back his arm and buried his fists in the man's ribs. He paused, surveyed his knuckles, then rocked back and kicked the helpless man in the gut.

By then, Nikki had seen enough.

"Heel," she said. She sprinted down the hill and across the open ground toward the buildings with Gunner by her side.

By the time they reached the back of barn three, Ana had run outside. She stood by her fallen friend who had curled in a protective ball, groaning in pain. The guard stood over him, his hands fisted. Drops of red spittle stained the ground, mixed with an upended plate of chicken and gravy.

"Stop!" Ana said, pulling ineffectually at the guard's arm. "*Por favor*. You're killing him."

"You were told to give up on that horse," the guard said. "I'm beginning to think you want more of this."

He made a lewd gesture at his crotch then backhanded her across the face.

Nikki was still ten feet away but a furious Gunner launched through the air. His mouth locked around the guard's arm, the force of his leap dragging the man against the wall.

The guard gave a shocked curse then fumbled beneath his jacket with his other hand. Nikki charged forward, twisted his wrist and jerked the gun from his hand.

She stepped back, checking the weapon. A Glock 19, compact but deadly, the feel of the pebbled handle as familiar as her toothbrush.

"What the fuck!" the guard yelled. "Get that dog off me."

"Quit," she said to Gunner, low and firm. He'd made his own decision to attack the man and she wasn't positive he'd listen. But Gunner released the man's arm and backed up two steps. His mouth was still curved in a snarl though and his raised hackles made him appear doubly ferocious.

"Dammit, this is private property," the guard said. He rose to his knees, his gaze switching from Gunner to Nikki. He didn't seem very intimidated by her jogging shorts and pink running shoes.

"You bitches are in big trouble," he said, full of bravado again. "And that dog is getting a bullet."

"Stop talking." Nikki raised both hands, leveled the Glock at him and stared over the sights. His mouth tightened and he turned silent.

She glanced at Ana. "This place isn't very employee friendly. You better leave with me."

Ana just stared, wide-eyed, the paleness of her face outlining the ugly imprint of the guard's knuckles on her cheek. Then she bent and clutched at the little man's arm.

"*Perdona,* Jorge," she said, helping him to his feet. "Are you okay?"

It appeared Jorge might have a couple cracked ribs, his nose was squashed, and the awkward way he moved didn't bode well for a six-mile hike. But not much could be done for broken ribs.

"We better get moving," Nikki said. There was still a security guard in the woods and it was unsettling not to know his location. "Do you have a car?"

"No car." Ana wrung her hands. "I only drive the farm vehicles. Besides, I can't leave Chico."

Gunner growled and Nikki's gaze shot back to the guard. He hadn't moved other than to give a smug smile. But clearly Gunner didn't like his attitude. Neither did she.

"What's the deal with Chico?" she asked. "Why can't you leave him?"

"He has a race tomorrow," Ana said. "If he wins, he's mine and we can go home to Chile. I can't give up now. Not after...everything."

Her gaze skittered from the guard to Jorge and then to her feet, and Nikki remembered Smitty's text about employee agreements. "Is that why you never leave Chico alone? I gather Durant doesn't want to lose the horse?"

Ana gave a tight nod. "For the last few months, it's been getting worse. Then Chico ran again and that made nineteen wins. One more and he's mine. That's when things turned very bad. All the other longtime grooms are gone. When our last friend refused to quit, his horse was hurt, so crippled he can never race again."

"How does hurting horses help Durant's income?"

"The horse is a stallion," Ana said. "Studs don't have to stay sound to make money. They only have to mount a mare. And Chico is a stallion too—"

"Believe me, lady," the guard growled. "You don't want to get involved with this."

Nikki frowned at his interruption. "But I don't understand why he wants Chico so badly," she said, talking to Ana but watching the guard. "He has plenty of other horses." And based on the signs over the stalls, those other horses had more illustrious breeding than Chico.

"A stallion syndicate made an offer," Ana said. "More than Durant ever expected. And his goal is to be a prominent breeder. To have his name respected in the industry."

"This is none of your damn business," the guard said. "Just put the gun down and I swear you won't get hurt." But his eyes shifted. He didn't like being on his knees and his promise was curdled with resentment.

"So you have a contract," Nikki said to Ana. "You own Chico if he wins twenty races. But how are you supposed to get him to the track?"

"The agreement gives permission to use a company truck and trailer for racing purposes."

"Where is this race tomorrow?"

"Riverview Racetrack, four hours south."

"Don't be stupid," the guard said. "There's no way that horse is going to win again." He looked at Ana, his voice malicious. "You'll be the reason he's crippled. And you know what happens when people get big ideas."

"Can you grab some rope, Ana," Nikki asked, tiring of this brute with his big fists and even bigger mouth. "Along with some leg wraps."

Ana didn't move. Her feet appeared rooted to the ground.

"These people are too chicken shit to help," the guard sneered, reaching for his cell phone. "And you won't shoot. Now you're screwed along with the two of them."

Gunner gave an ominous growl. His hackles were straight up, making him appear massive. Even Nikki was intimidated when he looked like that. The guard lowered his hand to the ground, deciding he didn't need to use his phone.

"Best not to move," she said. "Or talk. My dog doesn't listen well when he's riled." She spoke through tight lips, hating to imagine the abuse Ana had endured. The fact that the guard was still making threats showed the level of control Durant wielded.

"Don't worry about him, Ana," she went on, motioning toward the barn door. "Go and get what I asked. Hurry."

Ana shuffled back a step, then turned and raced around the corner of the barn.

She was back in minutes, carrying two horse bandages, a length of white rope and several lead lines. Her face was still unnaturally pale and her eyes were so wide they seemed to take up half her face. But she seemed more confident.

"I didn't know how you planned to use the rope," she said. "So I brought different thicknesses. The white one is better for tying. And the bandages aren't clean. In fact, I rolled them in manure."

Nikki grinned, glad to see the return of Ana's spunk. Durant hadn't been able to wipe that out.

"You're both dead," the man growled as Nikki tied his hands behind his back. But he kept his voice low, his eyes on Gunner. "Don't you dare stick that shitty bandage in my mouth, bitch."

"Watch your language." She gave his head a cuff, causing Gunner to jerk forward, his jaws gaping. He hadn't remained in his hold command but he let her wave him down. Clearly he was choosing when to listen, deciding on his own when she needed help. Not ideal but this wasn't the time to pause for a training lesson. And it helped keep the guard malleable, knowing Gunner was a loose cannon.

She finished gagging the man. His eyes were furious above the soiled bandage wrapped around his mouth but he didn't struggle. And now his curses were nicely muffled.

At least we know the gag works, Nikki thought, as she finished hogtying his feet. She removed his phone, resisting the urge to give him a kick in the ribs on Jorge's behalf. Besides, Gunner was poised close to the man's groin, just looking for a reason to attack, and the guard was helpless.

They were still in a precarious position. Gunner was fired up, Jorge was in pain and couldn't walk any distance, and Ana was hell-bent not to leave Chico.

"Let's grab a vehicle and get out of here," Nikki said. They probably didn't have much time before someone would come looking for the guard. And the man had made a phone call. "We'll get help and come back for Chico."

"No, they'll hurt him." Ana wrung her hands in anguish. "Durant already cut a couple horses' tendons."

Nikki blinked. That was almost too horrifying to believe. But the guard's eyes showed no surprise, only an annoying degree of complacency. Clearly he knew Durant was capable of such cruelty. And her heart ached to imagine Chico shuffling around his paddock, crippled, suitable for nothing except putting stud fees into his owners' pockets.

Durant was the polar opposite from Justin who made sure his horses received a comfortable retirement, regardless of their racing success. She certainly couldn't desert a vulnerable horse.

And bullies who willingly worked for sadists like Durant were despicable. She wanted to wipe the smugness off the guard's face, even if it was only temporary.

"Fine," she said to Ana. "Grab a truck and trailer. In the meantime, Gunner missed his supper. Good thing he's not fussy about the type of balls he chews." She stared meaningfully at the guard, gratified when his eyes widened and he jerked up his knees, trying to protect his genitals.

"It's okay, Gunner. Eat up."

She waited a long moment before motioning her dog past the guard, toward the spot on the ground that held the spilled chicken dinner, complete with peas, corn and gravy.

CHAPTER FIVE

Nikki peeked around the end door of the barn, checking Durant's house. Still no movement but they needed to leave his property, and quickly. She peered down the aisle but couldn't see Ana, only Jorge hunching against the wall.

She strode down the aisle and looked over the stall door. Ana had tied Chico in the corner and was painstakingly wrapping travel bandages around his lower legs.

"We don't have time for that," Nikki said, shaking her head. "Just lead him out and get him on the trailer."

"He can't ship without leg protection," Ana said, stubbornly continuing to wrap the right hind leg. "Not the night before a race. Besides, I'm almost finished."

She finally rose and stepped to the corner of the stall, scooped up her nylon travel bag and then untied Chico's lead rope.

"What about hay?" Nikki slid the stall door open, thinking the horse's food was way more important than wrapping his legs.

"There's hay and grain on the trailer," Ana said, passing Nikki her bag before leading Chico into the aisle where he immediately lowered his head to give Gunner a friendly sniff.

"You go first with the dog," Ana said. "Chico will feel better with the support."

Nikki glanced at Jorge who appeared to need more support than Chico. The horse seemed totally confident, ready to walk wherever Ana led him. Not surprising since she'd been with the horse since he was a yearling. On the other hand, Jorge seemed rather wobbly.

"Do you need any help, Jorge?" she asked.

He gave a dismissive head shake. "I won't hold you up," he said. "Just hurry."

At least he seemed to recognize the need for speed.

"Turn right outside the barn," Ana said, a note of authority still in her voice. She always seemed more assured around Chico. "We'll take the silver two-horse trailer. It's already hooked up."

Nikki strode from the barn and cut right, Gunner at her side. He was calm now, either not sensing danger or still content with his chicken dinner. Human food was always a treat. In fact, he looked downright happy, tail high, as if proud to be showing the way for this odd entourage.

Hopefully Chico would walk on the trailer without any fuss. A stubborn or excited horse could be a challenge to load. And create a lot of noise in the process—the type of sounds that would bring Durant's thugs running.

"That one." Ana pointed, quite unnecessarily as Jorge had moved past them to the rear door of a gleaming silver trailer, the smallest one in the lot.

He struggled to lower the ramp. Judging by his grimace he was in a lot of pain, but not the type to complain. Anyone who galloped racehorses for a living was accustomed to bumps and bruises.

Nikki stepped up and helped, nodding at his grateful smile. The ramp was relatively light and lowered with barely a squeak. So far, including a horse in their getaway hadn't caused much of a problem.

The first sign of trouble came from behind her—in the form of Chico's suspicious snort.

The horse had balked fifteen feet from the trailer. His head was high, his legs braced. Even Ana's firm tug on the lead line failed to coax him forward.

"Want me to tap him on the rump?" Nikki asked.

"That won't help," Ana said. "He just needs to make sure it's safe. He's not used to traveling by himself."

"He's a smart horse," Jorge said, his breathing still labored from the exertion. "He's learned to be careful around here. But he'll go on, eventually."

"How long is eventually?" Nikki asked.

Neither Ana nor Jorge answered. Even worse, they wouldn't look at her. Ana simply turned sideways, making soothing sounds and scratching Chico's shoulder while Jorge studied the toes of his scuffed boots.

"How long?" she repeated, a bite in her voice.

"Between fifteen and thirty minutes," Ana admitted. "But he's a fighter so it will end up taking longer if we push him. He doesn't respond well to force."

"Maybe we should get another horse to travel with him," Jorge said.

No time for that, Nikki thought. Nor was it wise. So far they hadn't done anything wrong other than defend themselves against a brutish guard. Ana had a contractual right to race Chico. But taking another horse would be stealing and she didn't want to give Durant any ammunition. The man seemed capable of anything and her gut instinct urged that they get off the property. Especially since he was so tight with the local police.

"Gunner," Nikki said, motioning at the trailer. "Go."

Gunner trotted up the rubber-covered ramp and sat beside a bulging hay net tied at the front of the trailer. He cocked his head, watching expectantly.

"Try leading him on now," Nikki said, keeping her voice calm, refraining from looking at Chico. As a green kid, she'd learned that if you make something into a big deal then so will the horse. So she stepped away from the ramp, forcing her body to relax, projecting a nonchalance she didn't feel.

Behind her, hooves thudded on the dirt, followed by a muffled sound as Chico walked up the rubber-matted ramp and joined Gunner in the trailer. Nikki eased forward, calmly hooked the butt rope and secured the rear door.

Jorge gave a triumphant thumbs-up, but it was too early to celebrate. They still had to get the horse to the track. Durant would be livid and he didn't seem the type to give up easily. He had money and men, and worse, a frightening lack of respect for others. Particularly women.

The only thing in their favor was that he probably didn't view them as worthy adversaries.

CHAPTER SIX

⸺◦⸺

Towing a horse trailer was surprisingly complicated. Nikki checked the truck's side mirror then glanced over at their driver. Ana's hands were white-knuckled over the wheel and she seemed determined to stay in the slow lane. Traffic whizzed past but the only quick things about Ana were her darting eyes. They swiveled back and forth, checking Jorge and Gunner in the back seat, Chico in the trailer, and Nikki in the passenger seat.

"You could go a little faster," Nikki said. "You know, just in case Durant and his men decide to chase us."

"But then the trailer will bump. Chico can't run his best if he's upset from his trip."

Nikki refrained from groaning. "Is he that sensitive?"

"He's the toughest, most easy-going Thoroughbred around," Ana said. "That's why American breeders are clamoring for his bloodlines. But horses are herd animals and tonight he's alone. Usually when we go to a race, he has another horse for company. This time is different."

"Guess we could have stuffed Durant's guard in the trailer with him," Nikki joked. They'd left the guard tied behind the barn. Hopefully he hadn't been discovered yet. At this speed a golf cart could catch them.

"That guard wouldn't make Chico feel better," Ana said. "He's fussy about his friends. And he needs to be in a good mood for his race."

Nikki accepted that nothing she said would make Ana speed up. The woman's priority was always Chico. That dedication was probably a big reason why the horse had stayed healthy and happy enough to win nineteen races. He still had to win one more time though, and if Ana thought he wouldn't like the trailer bouncing around, she was probably right.

Nikki pulled out her phone and clicked on the GPS, trying not to be alarmed at the low battery. She checked their bearings then turned it off, saving the remaining charge. But they were a sitting duck on this interstate.

"Take the next exit," she said, gesturing at the approaching ramp. "If they give chase, they'll be looking for us on the highway. And it's safer to drive slow on the secondary road...and better for Chico."

Ana hesitated then gave a grudging nod and eased off the interstate, driving as if she were hauling eggs.

Nikki bottled her edginess and glanced over the seat. "How are you feeling, Jorge?"

His face was bruised and his nose was probably broken although now it was his fear of Gunner that seemed to bother him the most. He pressed against the far side of the cab, looking uncomfortable but committed to keeping a safe distance from the dog.

"There's a hospital a few miles away," she added. "We can drop you off there."

He gave an emphatic shake of his head. "No, I am fine. Nothing is broken. Besides, that hospital is too close."

"Too close?"

"Mr. Durant has connections," Ana said. "Police, hospital, vets. He does whatever he wants. You surprised him today, calling the police, reporting that bone."

"So you know what Gunner found?" A chill ran down the back of Nikki's neck.

"I imagine it was some sort of bone," Ana said. "That's how he threatens us."

"But it appears to be human." Nikki twisted in the seat, studying Ana's expression, amazed the woman was so calm.

"There are horses buried on the property. There are lots of bones available."

"Is that why it was planted in the field? Was it intended to scare you?"

Ana nodded, her face pale in the dying light. "Up until a few months ago, Mr. Durant never bothered me. He didn't think it possible that Chico would keep winning. The average racehorse only has ten starts. But Chilean-bred horses are different. They're tough and can run more often. Breeders were beginning to notice and make offers.

"At first he was happy about Chico's rising value. But when Chico kept winning, his lawyers alerted him to the agreement and he realized he could lose ownership. That's when everything turned b-bad."

The quiver in Ana's voice proved she wasn't as calm as she first appeared. Clearly Durant had left his mark. There was a bruise on her slender neck and one of her fingers was deformed. Nikki gripped her hands on her lap, holding her questions, giving Ana time to regain her composure.

The rhythmic whir of the tires was soothing and finally Ana spoke again.

"When I didn't quit like the other grooms, the accidents turned more frequent. Chico's best friend, a retired gray gelding, was shot. Supposedly mistaken for a coyote. Another of Chico's buddies was electrocuted when a radio fell into his water bucket. The police wouldn't listen. I didn't dare leave him alone. Chico wasn't happy not being turned out each day so I took him to the paddock at the end of the property. And he kept on winning.

"Old Mr. Durant was a good man," she added. "He wanted to share his fortune. He brought in English teachers and helped us fill out the endless government forms. I worked for him a long time. But his son is the devil. He hired ruthless men who will do whatever he wants..." Her voice broke and she visibly gulped. "Three other workers are missing. Maybe they left the country. But now I am the only groom left with an ownership option."

"Do you have that agreement in writing? Somewhere safe?"

"Yes, I kept it in a plastic bag, hidden in the straw in Chico's stall. But now it is here, over my heart." Ana pulled a hand off the steering wheel and thumped her chest. "It's not safe to leave it anywhere."

A safety deposit box would be better, Nikki thought. However, Ana had shown she was a quick and pragmatic thinker, and so far she'd kept the contract safe.

"What about the bones?" Nikki asked. "Where does Durant get them?"

"There's a horse graveyard on the property."

"But what about the human arm?"

"*No sé*!" For an agitated moment Ana lifted her hands completely off the steering wheel. "Maybe the morgue. But I don't want to think about it!"

"Okay," Nikki said soothingly. They didn't need a traffic accident. She glanced back at Jorge but his mouth was set in a tight line, his expression almost as agonized as Ana's.

"Back to your agreement," Nikki said. "It would be better if you copied it and kept the original in a safety deposit box."

"But it's impossible to leave the property. I'm allowed to drive the truck and trailer but only for a race, and I can't leave Chico. I've been sleeping in his stall for the last month. If not for Jorge's help, and now yours—" She pulled her gaze from the road and shot Nikki a wobbly smile. "You aren't afraid to put yourself in danger. Even for strangers. That is unusual. Everyone else is scared."

Nikki shifted on the seat, uncomfortable with the gratitude. They hadn't made it to the track yet and the more she learned about Durant, the more her apprehension grew. It was comforting to feel the guard's Glock lying on the floor next to her foot.

"I'm happy to help," she said lightly. "I don't like Durant either. Besides, you were nice to Gunner when he needed it. And he really likes your horse."

"Yes," Ana said. "Gunner and Chico are both brave and bighearted. Warriors and soul mates."

Nikki glanced back at her dog, thinking that Ana sounded a bit like Sonja. Gunner thumped his tail against the seat, his eyes bright. He leaned against the side of the rear cab, as if aware Jorge wasn't comfortable with his presence.

"Soul mates or not," Nikki said, straightening in her seat, "at least we all got out of there."

"But Mr. Durant will follow," Ana said.

"You're allowed to drive the trailer though. So it's not like you're doing anything wrong. And he has lots of other horses. Maybe he'll let Chico run his race. It might be too much trouble to chase you."

Even to Nikki, that view sounded overly optimistic. Clearly Durant was a vindictive man, one who was accustomed to getting his own way. It was courageous—and foolhardy—for Ana to have stood up to him for so long. Especially considering the man's threats. And it was all because of a little brown horse that looked no different than any other animal in the field. In fact, Chico resembled the common horses Nikki had ridden as a kid rather than a flashy racehorse.

"How much would Chico cost?" she asked. "Maybe you could buy him?"

Ana sighed. "I wish he wasn't so valuable. Now it's impossible. The last offer was up to fourteen."

"Fourteen thousand?"

"Fourteen million."

Nikki pressed back in her seat, almost choking on her surprise. They were pulling a friendly brown horse that looked like a backyard pet. He certainly wasn't as eye-catching as Justin's horses. But the bay Thoroughbred tucked in the trailer was worth over fourteen million bucks. People killed for less.

She jerked forward, studying the dark road. "There's a pothole to your right."

Ana eased around the rut then shot Nikki an appreciative look, approving of the newfound concern for giving Chico a smooth ride.

Nikki gave a sheepish smile. But her mind was whirling. Now she had no doubt that Durant would follow. And that he'd go to considerable lengths to stop them. Would he force the trailer off the road? Probably not. He clearly didn't place much value on human lives but he wouldn't risk killing his horse.

"Does Durant need Chico alive?" she asked. "Or is there an insurance policy?"

"All the horses are insured for their purchase price or the value of the races where they are competing. But Chico's real value is at stud. He doesn't have to be race sound, only able to breed. Mr. Durant wants him alive but he doesn't care about his health, only the money he will bring." Ana's voice thickened. "He had a special breeding ramp built, so crippled stallions can still cover mares."

Nikki winced. So it would be best for Durant if Chico was able to take care of stud duties but made unfit for future racing. That would leave Ana's agreement useless. Durant Sr. may have wanted to provide incentives. However, his death had created a toxic environment for the horses, as well as the workers.

"I'm surprised you're still in one piece," she said slowly. "Chico too."

"Mr. Durant knew I was helpless," Ana said. "He demanded I rip up my contract. Jorge and I wanted to take Chico and leave, but he was always watching."

"Where would you go?"

"Back to Chile. Then I'd post my contract on social media and tell everyone about the things Durant has done. He'd hate having his racing image wrecked. We knew we had to get Chico out before he was hurt. We thought about riding him into the state park and hiding him somewhere safe. I found a few boarding barns but they were too far to reach on foot."

Nikki remembered the armed man posted by the park trail, and her blood chilled. It was unlikely Ana would have made it off the property.

"But then you and Gunner showed up," Ana went on. "And helped us escape."

"We still have to make it to the track."

"Yes." Ana pulled in a ragged breath, "And Chico still has to win...one more time."

CHAPTER SEVEN

An hour later, they were rolling along a narrow secondary road flanked by deer grass and reflective road signs. The sun had set and the shroud of darkness was comforting. There were many routes into Riverview Racetrack and it would be difficult for Durant to cover them all.

Gunner pressed his nose into Nikki's arm and gave an insistent whine.

"We need to stop soon for a break," she said.

"But it's only fifty more miles," Ana said, her gaze dropping to the illuminated dashboard. "All the work vehicles are kept gassed up so we have enough fuel."

"Gunner needs to pee. Jorge needs pain meds. And I need to pick up some dog food, and something for us as well. Unless the track sells food?"

"I forgot that you went for a morning jog," Ana said. "And haven't eaten all day. But you won't be able to enter the track. Neither will Gunner. Only companion animals like pigs and goats are allowed. Can you call your boyfriend? Have him pick you up and take you back to your car?"

"Justin's busy for the next couple days. But you said Chico likes company when he's traveling. We'll just explain that Gunner keeps him calm."

"No. He might make too much noise and scare the horses."

"Gunner doesn't bark," Nikki said. "Not unless it's important."

Admittedly, sometimes he made his own decisions around aggressive men, but she didn't plan on mentioning that. Track security probably wouldn't even notice a dog in the back seat. When she went to the races with Justin, they were waved through the owners' gate with minimal fuss.

She didn't want to desert Ana and Jorge. Besides, it would be fun to see Chico run. Watching Justin's horses had always been fun, but the outcome had never been critical. Of course she'd enthusiastically cheered them on, but a two-dollar bet didn't measure up to Ana's high stakes.

Thinking of Justin reminded her that she hadn't updated him in a while. She sent him another text, knowing he'd be immersed in his court case but feeling a measure of comfort that he knew her location. And Ana's race plan.

Her phone screen flashed with his return message. *Didn't realize you were so tight with Ana. Chaos here. Looks like judge is going to throw out critical evidence. Will be meeting with prosecutor all weekend. Have fun at the track. Talk later.*

Short and succinct. She fought a little pang. But he wasn't the type to add heart emojis. Besides, she didn't want to go into long explanations about Durant and cause unnecessary worry. Justin had already helped so much with her career. Even if he had the time to talk, her phone battery was too low to burn on conversation. Texts used less power. She finished with another message to Sonja, explaining that her arrival would be delayed until Saturday night.

"Do either of you have an iPhone charger?" she asked, eyeing her orange battery indicator.

Ana shook her head and Jorge merely grunted so she flipped open the glove compartment. She rummaged through its contents but found no charger, only documents including Ana and Jorge's track credentials along with another groom's laminated pass.

She scanned the woman's ID: a female groom named Gloria Cortes. It might be possible to pass for Gloria in a pinch, although the woman had dark hair and Nikki's was more auburn. There were also papers showing vehicle registration, proof of insurance, a melted protein bar...along with scores of condoms.

"Wow, someone was expecting a bit of action," she teased. She hadn't realized Ana and Jorge were a couple. Clearly they were loyal friends but she hadn't picked up on any sexual vibes. There was also quite an age difference although they did share an obvious love of horses.

She shoved everything back in the glove compartment and clicked it shut, smiling at Ana. But neither Ana nor Jorge replied, their silence brittle.

"Sorry," Nikki said. "Didn't mean to make you uncomfortable. Sex is a great thing."

"The condoms don't belong to us," Ana said, her voice toneless. "Mr. Durant put them there. He does what he wants, knowing we can't refuse. One of the reasons he hires illegals."

Bile rose in Nikki's throat, her revulsion overriding any words. Back at the stable, the guard had made a lewd comment and gestured at his crotch. Now it made sense.

"If we resisted," Ana went on, "his men were allowed to join in. A perk of the job. I think that's the reason Gloria left. She was young and pretty. And way too feisty."

Nikki pressed against the back of the seat, her body so tight all she could do was stare at the road ahead. She'd already learned that if Ana had more to say, the words would come easier if given time.

But this was horrifying. Ana and her friends would have had no place to turn, no protection from the ongoing abuse. And Nikki had a special grudge with people who preyed on vulnerable women. She still ached for what her sister had endured at the hands of a man they'd trusted.

She crossed her arms, working hard to sound as calm as Ana. "We can't let him get away with this. I'll hire a lawyer who will take your statement. And from any other women who are brave enough to step forward. He's a sadist, a rapist and possibly a murderer."

"No!" The vehemence in Ana's voice was startling.

"A court case is too long," Ana added. "Too expensive. And many workers are undocumented. Besides, Durant will claim the sex was consensual. And he will provide witnesses. He's already warned us."

Nikki squeezed her eyes shut. Undeniably, it would be an uphill fight, especially for workers whose main goal was to remain in America. The threat of deportation made it hard to ask authorities for help.

"What about the severed arm?" Nikki said. "It had to come from someone."

"Probably not from anyone I know. And maybe it was from the morgue. He controls the entire area."

"But Durant's a predator. We can't let him win."

"For me, it's a win if I can take Chico home."

"What about your friends?"

"They're all gone. Only a few older women are left and Durant won't bother them. Especially since they don't have ownership options."

"But I can help," Nikki said. "With your legal fees, anything. Whatever you need."

"Thanks, but no. The court can't change what has happened. And owning Chico will make everything worthwhile."

"But predators need to be stopped. Punished."

"This is my choice," Ana said, speaking with quiet dignity. "And I'm not like you, caring so much for justice."

Nikki pressed her lips together, accepting the truth in Ana's words. Investigative work wasn't only a job. Her sister's murder had turned it into a calling. Not only did she want to help people; she liked to see their offenders punished.

"But we can get Durant," she said, trying one last time. "I have a picture of the arm. Let me take some shots of your bruises, Jorge's injuries—"

"No! Justice isn't my goal. And I won't let anger affect my actions."

Nikki folded her arms. Ana sounded a lot like Sonja who believed Gunner didn't listen because he no longer trusted her judgment. And maybe anger did color her decisions, especially when it was the only way to make criminals pay. She certainly didn't understand how Justin remained confident in the law, especially when it favored the wealthy and was usually too ponderous to give much satisfaction.

Bright lights of a service station split the darkness, pulling back her attention. Its sprawling parking lot was filled with cars. To the side, sat several transport trucks along with a white horse trailer.

She gestured, still shaken by Ana's revelations. "Pull in and park on the left," she said. "On the other side of the white horse trailer. I'll take Gunner behind the building where nobody can see." Not only was he a distinctive shepherd but he was unusually big. No sense making it easy for Durant's minions to report a sighting.

"Do you have a screwdriver?" she asked.

"There's a tool kit in the trailer," Ana said. "Along with water and buckets if you want to give Gunner a drink. I'll go inside and grab some sandwiches."

"Don't use a credit card."

Ana lifted a wry eyebrow. "I don't own a credit card. Only cash. And I expect you want to choose the dog food yourself. Some of them contain nothing but fillers."

Nikki nodded, appreciating the empathy of a fellow animal lover. Ana understood how owners worried about their dog's food. And thought it completely reasonable.

Ana leaned closer to the steering wheel and eased into the parking lot. There was plenty of space between the transport truck and horse trailer but it took her several attempts to park, inching forward and backward multiple times. Finally she turned off the ignition, satisfied with her parking job.

"Do you need to get out, Jorge?" Nikki peered into the back seat, her hand already gripping the door handle.

He shook his head, a relief since his bruised face would likely draw attention. Exactly what they didn't want.

"Okay," she said. "Then stay inside and keep the doors locked."

She gestured at Gunner who leaped from the back seat and onto the pavement. He trotted to the rear of the vehicle, lifted his leg and peed on the tire. There'd be no need to walk him behind the building after all.

Ana hurried past him and opened the side door of the trailer. Chico gave a welcoming nicker, his ears locked on Gunner. Ana felt his chest with the back of her hand and gave Nikki a satisfied smile. "He's traveling well," she said. "Not hot or upset. He's glad to see your dog."

Nikki edged sideways so Gunner could enter the trailer. He did have a calming effect on animals, and on her as well—at least when she wasn't worrying about him turning aggressive.

Gunner leaped up beside Chico, tail wagging. His tongue was hanging out though, and he was clearly thirsty. No doubt Chico was too. The night was cooling but it had been a hot day.

"Where's the water?" Nikki glanced around, trying to keep Ana moving. "And the screwdriver?"

Ana moved to a compartment next to Chico and pulled out a tool kit and a travel bucket along with a huge container of water. She filled the bucket, offering the water to Chico first who sipped daintily. When he lifted his nose from the bucket, Gunner licked his dripping muzzle. Chico lowered his head further, either liking the sensation of Gunner's tongue or else trying to share the water.

Ana laughed and set the bucket down for Gunner who noisily lapped for over a minute.

"Chico has better table manners than Gunner," Nikki said, smiling at the horse and dog. They'd become good friends. Other than her pony, she'd never seen Gunner lick another animal's face.

"At first I was worried about his teeth so close to Chico," Ana admitted. "But your dog is very gentle."

Usually, Nikki thought, watching him lie down by Chico's feet and contentedly lick his paws. Above him, Chico pulled at his hay with renewed vigor, obviously happy to have the dog's company.

"I'll leave Gunner in the trailer while we go inside," she said. "He can stretch out better and will be out of sight."

Ana nodded and closed the door. Nikki waited until it was secure then strode to the back of the trailer, screwdriver in hand.

"What are you doing?" Ana called.

"Switching license plates. Just in case. Go in the gas bar and buy some sandwiches and bottled water. And some painkiller for Jorge. When you see me in there, act like you don't know me."

"All right," Ana said, her voice turning solemn. She turned and hurried off, her slight figure dwarfed by the looming transport truck.

It took longer than expected to switch plates between the two trailers. Some of the screws were rusted in place. The horse inside pawed and kicked the wall, rocking the trailer, and it was obvious he wasn't as calm as Chico. He seemed to think she'd arrived to take him off the trailer and when that hadn't happened, he was vigorously demonstrating his displeasure.

"Sorry, buddy," she murmured, struggling with the last screw, guessing that the owner of the horse was in the restaurant enjoying a sit-down meal. Otherwise someone would have popped up, checking on the ruckus.

She secured the second plate, stuck the screwdriver in her pocket then followed a bickering family of five into the station. The convenience store was to the right; Ana's head was visible by the fast food section. Nikki circled in the opposite direction, toward the grocery shelves.

There were only two types of dog food and neither brand was familiar. She scooped one up, peering at the fine print, trying to decipher the ingredients.

"My dog likes that one," a man behind her said. "It's handy in a pinch."

She glanced over her shoulder. A good-looking guy in a ball cap stood behind her. He had a coffee in one hand and a phone strapped to his belt. He gave a friendly smile, his gaze sweeping her face.

"Nice to know," she said.

"I usually feed raw," the man went on. "But it's hard when I'm trucking. And the gas stations always carry that brand. But some dogs get sick when food is changed suddenly. What kind of dog do you have?"

"Yes, it's best not to switch too much," she murmured, ignoring his last question.

"Are you traveling? Need to grab something quick?"

"No, just looking," Nikki said, placing the food back on the shelf. The guy was a little too friendly and this wasn't the time to strike up a conversation. She wanted to get in and out without anyone remembering her.

She moved several feet along the aisle but the trucker followed, still talking about dogs and breeds, and how it got lonely on the road. She stopped in front of the feminine products, pretending a keen interest in the selection of tampons. He hesitated then lost interest and drifted away.

She quickly returned to the dog food. Ana and Jorge probably didn't have a lot of money so she scooped up the cheaper bag then joined Ana in the fast food aisle. She set the bag close to Ana's feet and detoured to the bathroom.

The warm soapy water felt good and it was refreshing to wash away the grime. She peered into the mirror, using a paper towel to blot her face dry. The messy ponytail and running clothes made her look as if she'd just finished a marathon. It was surprising the trucker had even thought she wanted to chat, let alone be open to a pickup.

He probably wasn't even a trucker. His clothes had been a little too crisp and his light pants weren't the usual choice for a long haul. Even his shoes were clean, a soft brown leather that didn't show a trace of road dust. No doubt just a lonely guy looking for some conversation, making up questions, pretending to care about what breed of dog she owned.

Her hand froze midair as realization swept her. Then she wheeled away from the sink, slammed the wadded paper in the garbage bin and bolted out the door.

CHAPTER EIGHT

A na had finished at the cash register and stood outside, the bag of purchases tucked under her arm. Nikki charged past, scanning the parking lot. Their truck and trailer were still there, untouched. But the horse trailer beside them looked different—its back door was wide open.

Ana followed her gaze. "Oh, no! Durant found us!" she said, lurching forward.

"Quiet." Nikki grabbed her arm, slowing Ana down. "Walk normal. We might be able to drive away. He thinks Chico is in the trailer beside us."

She kept a comforting grip of Ana's elbow, guiding her to the left of the parked trucks. They edged around the big rigs, ducking between a white tractor-trailer and a refrigerated van, their steps soundless on the pavement. Soon they were less than twenty feet from their truck.

The man from the dog food aisle stood behind the adjacent trailer, the silhouette of his ball cap outlined by the glaring overhead lights. His cell phone was pressed to his ear.

"License plate matches," he said. "But the horse inside is gray, not brown. And the trailer is a four-horse, not a two. The woman inside fits your description though. She was looking at dog food. But she seems to be traveling alone."

He was silent for a moment, then nodded. "Yeah, okay. There's a silver horse trailer here. I'll check that out and call you back."

Nikki pressed Ana against the bumper, raised a finger to her mouth and slipped around the front of their truck to the passenger's door...and to the Glock tucked beneath the seat.

She eased the handle up. But the door wouldn't open and she gave a silent groan. It was locked, just as she'd instructed Jorge.

Rising on her toes, she pressed her face against the side window and peered in.

Jorge's mouth was open, his head twisted against the back of the cab. Her breath jammed in horror. Then she saw his chest rise, heard his relaxed snores. Not dead, only sleeping. But he certainly wasn't going to unlock the door, and the man would hear any rapping on the glass.

She felt for the screwdriver in her pocket and steadied her breathing. Not much of a weapon but at least it was something. She crept around the bumper of the truck, edging closer to their trailer.

The man in the ball cap was already lifting the bolts on the back of Chico's trailer door. The sound jarred the night but he seemed unconcerned about making any noise.

He lowered the ramp and she could see the light of his phone as he scanned the interior. The trailer vibrated, followed by a deep-throated snarl. Then the man stumbled backward with a hundred pounds of protective dog at his chest.

"Quit," Nikki called, rushing forward.

The man was flat on his back, legs flailing, one arm pressed over his throat. She ran up beside Gunner, grabbed his collar and pulled him back. "Quit," she repeated, keeping a tight grip, hoping she could control him.

"What the hell!" the man said.

"What are you looking for?"

"Nothing, I just couldn't remember where I parked."

"And you couldn't remember if you were hauling a horse trailer?"

"It happens. Not an offense. And your dog scared the shit out of me." His voice strengthened and he sat up, fumbling over the pavement for his phone.

"Don't move," she said.

"Don't tell me what to do. I'm calling animal control. Your dog attacked with no reason. Animals like that shouldn't be loose on public property."

"He wasn't loose," she said, watching the man continue to feel around for his phone. "But he might be soon."

The man stilled.

"What are you looking for?" she repeated.

He didn't answer.

She made a show of tightening both hands around Gunner's collar even though he hadn't moved a muscle. Gunner obligingly growled.

"A horse," the man said quickly. "A brown Thoroughbred called Chico."

"Why?"

"He was stolen. The owner doesn't want the police involved because it's a long-time employee. I'm supposed to call if I spot the horse."

"Then what?"

"I don't know. I make the call and get five thousand dollars."

Nikki stepped back, glancing warily around the parking lot. This man didn't know anything about horses, or the true situation. He wasn't even one of Durant's trained goons; he just wanted to make some quick cash. No telling how many other people were in receipt of the same offer. Apparently they were in a different police jurisdiction so Durant couldn't rely on his crooked authorities to track them down. Now he was using civilians.

She pulled out her most charming smile. "So you thought I stole a horse. How bizarre. Lady isn't even a Thoroughbred. She's a quarter horse, a barrel racer."

"I thought the offer was too good to be true." The man gave a rueful shrug. "This is the fifth horse trailer I've checked in the last half hour. And you do have a dog."

"How many of the other trailers had dogs?"

"Half of them," the man admitted, straightening his ball cap. "Is it okay if I pick up my phone now?"

"Sure," she said, keeping a friendly smile pasted on her face. "And I hope you find what you're looking for. But I would think thieves in a hurry would stick to the interstate."

"Yeah." He scooped up his phone and slid it in his shirt pocket. "I'm going to switch my location. All the trailers here are coming from the local horse show."

"Well, good luck. I'm going to close this door up and get my old girl home. She's always tired after a show."

"I'll help you lift the ramp," the man said, scrambling up from the ground. "Sorry if I scared you. Maybe I can make it up? Come by and watch your next show? Maybe buy you lunch?"

"That'd be nice," Nikki said, reaching down for her side of the ramp. Her hands closed around the steel handle just as Ana charged from the gloom.

"Don't close it," Ana called, clearly thinking the danger was past. "I want to check him."

Nikki shot her a warning look but Ana was focused on Chico. She stepped onto the trailer, paused at the horse's head, then crouched and checked all four legs. "Chico's fine," she said, not seeming to realize she'd called the horse by name.

The man stiffened and it was obvious he'd heard. When he looked back at Nikki, he was smiling again. But this time it was rather ugly.

"So you're not a barrel racer," he said. "Just a horse thief."

"We're not stealing this horse," Nikki said. "We have his papers."

"But it's a lot of money." The man's hand was already sliding into his pocket, feeling for his phone. "So I don't really care who owns him. I'm sure you'll understand why I have to call this in."

"And I'm sure you'll understand why we can't let you."

"We?" The man gave a cocky laugh. "Two women. Not much you can do."

She was getting rather tired of the misogynistic men she'd met today. "Gunner," she said, motioning with her hand. "Watch."

Gunner surged forward, lip curling over gleaming white teeth.

"Drop your phone on the ground," Nikki said. "And step into the trailer next to us."

The man didn't move, his eyes darting between Chico and Gunner. A person could take a lot of risks for five thousand dollars.

"Step into the trailer," she snapped. "This dog flunked out of K9 training. But not before he learned the best way to hurt a man. You're really much safer in there."

Gunner gave another menacing growl and tugged against his collar. The man took a jerky step back, then set his phone on the pavement and climbed into the adjacent trailer.

"Stay quiet," she said. "I'm going to leave the dog outside. We'll be back in half an hour to pick him up. After we deliver the horse. But if you open the door before that, unfortunately I won't be around to call him off..."

"Watch," she said to Gunner. He charged past her to stand stiff legged behind the trailer, hackles up, lips curled in a snarl. Even Ana edged away. The man scrambled to the front of the trailer, squeezing close to a gray gelding who was unimpressed by the strange human. The gray pinned his ears and slammed the wall with his hind feet, the sound reverberating through the parking lot.

Nikki closed the door, made a show of talking loudly to Gunner, telling him to stay and guard. Then she motioned for him to follow her to the truck.

Ana banged on the side window, rousing Jorge enough to unlock the doors. They clambered into the cab with Gunner leaping into the back seat, pausing only to give Jorge's face a swift lick on the way by.

"That little charade won't give us much more than five minutes," Nikki said. "So we need to hurry. It's best if I drive."

"Have you hauled horses before?"

Nikki crossed her arms. It couldn't be that hard and at least she would drive a lot faster. But Ana was waiting as if the answer was important and she couldn't lie to the woman. "I've driven a lot of different vehicles," she said. "In a lot of situations."

"But you've never pulled a horse trailer? Or ridden in the back to see how bumpy it is?"

"No."

"Then I will continue to drive."

"But you have to go faster," Nikki said. "Now we know they're coming. At least the police aren't chasing us, only Durant and whoever he's paying."

She glanced over her shoulder. Jorge was yawning, oblivious to the drama. He was still so groggy he didn't seem to notice that Gunner was pressed against his side, bright-eyed and stoked from the recent action.

But Gunner had listened, even under pressure. Although the man hadn't been much of a physical threat. Maybe Sonja was correct in believing that Gunner decided when aggression was needed and that he no longer entirely trusted her judgment. She had no idea how to prove herself to her dog though, other than to keep her own emotions in check. And that was easier said than done.

"I'm sorry about screwing up back there," Ana said humbly. "I was worried about Chico and getting him to the track healthy."

"It's fine," Nikki said. "You did great. But you could help by driving faster."

Ana pressed on the gas pedal and the engine throbbed, eager to respond. The truck had lots of power. They just needed to use it.

Nikki leaned over, checking the illuminated dashboard. Their speed had increased but it was still well under the posted limit. Ana's worry about Chico not being bumped around might prove irrelevant. Durant didn't know their current whereabouts, but he certainly knew their destination. He'd have plenty of time to cut them off. He could even sit outside the track and wait.

"Is there more than one entrance to the track?" she asked.

Ana shook her head. "Horsemen all use the back gate. There's a booth where they check the horse's papers. The guard makes sure they're entered in an upcoming race and have all their required shots. That's where they'll check our creds."

"So for sure I won't be able to get in?"

"Definitely not. But Jorge will be bringing the trailer back outside the gate once we drop off Chico. He can drive you to a motel. Or maybe you and Gunner could sleep in the truck? It's not fancy but we have lots of horse blankets."

Nikki palmed her phone. She didn't need fancy. Besides, she had no credit cards or ID and she was reluctant to call Justin and ask him to pay for a motel. He'd question the situation. And then worry about her when he should be concentrating on his testimony.

It might also be difficult to find a dog friendly motel. Or any motel for that matter. The last four they'd passed had posted No Vacancy signs.

"I'd be happy to sleep in the truck," she said. "Just drop me off outside the gate, close to where Jorge will park. Then tomorrow when the track opens to the public, I can get in and see Chico's race."

"You'll stay around and watch?" The relief in Ana's voice was heartwarming.

"Absolutely. I'm looking forward to it."

Besides, she couldn't walk away from Ana and Jorge. They had no other support. And the more she learned about Durant, the more obvious it was that he was both powerful and vindictive. Even more disturbing was that he didn't seem to have any qualms about the amount of pain he would inflict.

CHAPTER NINE

Nikki kept an alert eye on her side mirror, noting the string of vehicles hampered by Ana's tortoise pace. Most cars roared past whenever there was a chance. However one set of headlights stubbornly maintained its position.

Maybe the guy she'd stuffed in the horse trailer had figured it was safe to open the door and make a phone call. The shape of the vehicle fit an Escalade and its projector beam lights were distinctive. But it was hard to tell if it was actually tailing them or just content to mosey along. There were other Escalades on the road. Didn't mean it was from the Durant stable.

"Pull over a bit," she said. "Let some of this traffic get by."

Five vehicles seized the chance to swoop past, one with a grateful honk of its horn. However, the Escalade reduced its speed, keeping pace with their truck.

"What are you watching?" Ana asked. "Does the trailer have a flat?" She jammed her foot on the brake, causing the car on their bumper to flick their lights in annoyance.

"Everything's fine," Nikki said. "Keep driving normal. But we have company, a couple cars back."

Ana pressed the gas pedal.

"Drive normal," Nikki repeated, feeling with her foot for the gun on the floor. "They've been following for a while. There's too much traffic for them to try anything here."

Their complacent tail also indicated Durant thought he had plenty of time to stop Chico from running. Whatever he planned would likely happen once they hit a more deserted section.

She angled against the seat, her gaze locked on the SUV in the mirror, wishing once again that she was behind the wheel. Ana's driving skills were questionable although the Glock gave some comfort. Hopefully the gun wouldn't be required.

They drove another thirty miles, past 24-hour fast food restaurants, tourist attraction signs and garishly lit strip malls. The road remained busy. If anything, traffic increased.

A subdued row of lights twinkled in the distance. "That's the track," Ana said, her shoulders slumping in relief. "We made it."

Nikki peered through the windshield, amazed they'd reached the track without some sort of encounter. The Escalade had never moved closer than two car lengths. And that didn't make sense.

Ana veered to the right, clearly familiar with the horsemen's entrance. They passed a parking lot reserved for trailers and edged into a line of vehicles awaiting entry to the track.

"That's where Jorge will meet you after we unload Chico," Ana said, gesturing at the gravel lot. "Spectator gates open tomorrow at eleven so you'll be able to get admission then. I'll let you out near the security gate. Jorge will be back for you in less than an hour."

She went on to talk about blankets and truck heaters and how the night shouldn't be too cold but Nikki's concerns still revolved around Durant. He knew Chico's destination; he must have something planned. Right now he seemed to be toying with them. Perhaps he found it creepily entertaining, like a cat playing with a mouse.

She checked her mirror again but couldn't spot the Escalade. And that left her even more uneasy.

"You're sure this is the only entrance to the barn area?" she asked.

"Yes. The only one for vehicles."

"It would be better if Gunner and I were able to stay close to Chico. It doesn't seem likely that Durant has given up."

Ana tugged at her lower lip. "Probably not. And of course I'd like your protection. But it's impossible for you to get on the backstretch without creds."

Nikki opened the glove compartment and pulled out the three sets of credentials. "Then just call me Gloria," she said.

"We can't do that!"

"Why not? The guard probably won't check too closely. If it doesn't work, what's the harm? I'll just walk back to the parking lot and wait for Jorge."

"She does look a bit like Gloria," Jorge said, speaking up from the back seat. His arm was propped on Gunner's back and he looked more comfortable with both the dog and his pain. The meds and sleep had done wonders.

"But they might catch us." Ana nervously tapped her fingers on the steering wheel. "And then Chico would be suspended. I don't want anything to mess up his chance to run."

"He has to make it to the starting gate first," Nikki said. "And you have bigger problems than pleasing track security."

"It's too risky," Ana said. "This track is very strict. They wouldn't like us using false credentials."

"So you think Durant followed you all the way here just to turn around and go home? Isn't he the bigger risk?"

Ana wiggled in her seat then gave a reluctant nod, her gaze sliding back to Nikki. "Can you pull your hair out of the ponytail? Hide your face a bit?"

Nikki tugged off the elastic and fluffed her hair. "How's that?"

"Better," Ana said. "It might work. But how do we hide Gunner?"

"We can put him in the trailer with Chico."

"No, they'll check there. They need to make sure the horse matches his papers and vaccination records."

"Then he can lie on the floor," Nikki said. "Gunner can make himself very small when he curls up. We can even put a blanket over him."

Ana shook her head. "No, if they spot him, it will look like I'm doing something wrong. Then they might refuse Chico admission."

So it was all about getting caught, Nikki thought wryly. Using Gloria's ID was illegal, but to Ana it seemed more likely to work. However, she wasn't going anywhere without Gunner. The guard might not notice a dog lying on the floor. But if he did, at least they weren't trying to hide him and Ana could plead ignorance to the rule.

"We'll just try putting him on the floor then," Nikki said agreeably. "No blanket." Turning, she motioned him off the back seat.

Jorge shifted his legs to make more room and Gunner reluctantly left the cushioned seat and moved to the hard floor. His resigned groan made Jorge chuckle. Sharing the rear cab had turned them into travel buddies, something she hadn't anticipated, considering Jorge's initial fear.

"Stay down, Gunner," she said. If her phone had more charge, she would have snapped a picture of Jorge and Gunner and forwarded it to Justin. He'd be surprised to see how quickly Gunner had accepted a strange man.

Ahead of them, brake lights flickered, coloring the night with a reddish glow. The line inched forward, with a guard inspecting each horse, reinforcing that the track took its security seriously.

At last, there was only one trailer in front of them—an extravagant stretch limo for equines, spacious enough to hold a score of horses. If a Thoroughbred's speed could be judged by their transport, the horses in front of them were much faster than Chico.

"Does everyone haul in the night before a race?" Nikki asked, admiring the gleaming rig.

"No," Ana said. "Most horses are stabled on the grounds. But those who have their own training facility prefer to haul in."

"Looks like that trailer came from Santa Anita," Nikki said, studying the prominent stickers on the back. "They have good horses there."

"*Si poh*. That's where Durant wants to race."

Nikki had noted that Ana often reverted to her native language when she was excited so she remained silent, guessing she would keep talking.

"He wants to own horses that can win at those big tracks," Ana went on. "To him, image is everything. If one of his homebreds made it to the Kentucky Derby, or even the Santa Anita Derby, he'd be ecstatic. Especially since his father was never able to win at the upper tier tracks. But Durant didn't even realize Chico's potential until the breeding syndicates made their offers. Now he's desperate to keep him."

"But you only have to win one more race. And then you own him. And it's an easy one tomorrow, right? If it's at a smaller track like Riverview?"

"No race is easy."

"Will any of those horses be in Chico's race?" Nikki asked, warily eyeing the commercial trailer in front of them.

"Yes. Chico only runs in top races."

"But he has to win. Why didn't you enter him in an easier one?"

"That's out of my control. I'm licensed as the groom and trainer, but Mr. Durant makes all the decisions."

Naturally Durant had put him in a tough race, Nikki thought. "Is Chico outclassed? Does he have any chance of winning?"

Ana's fingers lifted from the steering wheel then tightened again. "Every horse has a chance. That's why racing is full of surprises. Chico has a big heart. He'll understand the race is important. He'll try his best."

Nikki pressed back against her seat. She'd assumed the hardest part was getting the horse to the track. She hadn't thought about the race itself. And Chico might be kind, smart and devoted to Ana. But that didn't mean he'd cross the finish line first.

She squeezed the edge of her seat, trying to remember all the different types of races. The lowest were claiming, followed by allowance and handicap then graded stakes. Justin had owned some nice horses but he'd only won a few graded stakes. Which didn't bode well for Chico's chances.

Or Ana's. She certainly couldn't return to Durant's stable. Jorge either. It seemed like their problems were only mushrooming.

"What will you do if Chico doesn't win?" Nikki asked, keeping the alarm from her voice. "Try again? Can you enter him in an easier race? Maybe stay here where it's safe and run next week?"

"It wouldn't be fair to ask him to run with only a week's rest. Some Thoroughbreds need months between races. Chico needs to have grass and recharge, mentally and physically."

"But he might not make it to another race. As long as you have that contract, he's not safe."

"I'm not giving up my contract." Ana's mouth set in a stubborn line. "Old Mr. Durant would be happy that Chico is doing well. A little horse from Chile with almost twenty lifetime wins. And now he's seven years old and competing against top class horses."

Something about the way she said "competing" left Nikki even more uneasy. "Has he raced against top horses before?"

Ana gave a vigorous nod. "Yes, he's had some big races. Not many lately. Actually just one stakes this year. That was when Mr. Durant realized Chico should not win again. Or else he'd be mine."

"And where did Chico finish? In that stakes race?"

"Second to last," Ana admitted.

Nikki exhaled, long and slow. The sound was so loud in the cab that Jorge leaned forward, poking his head over the front seat.

"Chico is training well," he said. "I exercise him every day and he's in excellent shape."

"That's reassuring," Nikki said. But Gunner was also in good shape. Didn't mean he could beat a greyhound. Unless the greyhound was old or fat, and carried a lot of extra weight. She pictured the lead panels some of Justin's jockeys added to their saddle pads. Those evened out the field, especially for longer races.

"What about assigned weight?" she asked hopefully. "Is there some sort of handicap? Does Chico have to carry as much?"

"This isn't that type of race," Ana said. "Actually Chico might end up carrying a few more pounds than the others. The last race his jockey came in overweight."

Nikki gripped the seat even tighter. Understandably, it was hard for jockeys to stay below one hundred and eighteen pounds, especially in these modern times. People were simply bigger. A conditioned athlete had to make great sacrifices to meet their required weight, no matter their stature. Still, it would be helpful if Chico's jockey dropped a few pounds before his race.

She leaned forward, peering into the gloom beyond the gate, hoping to spot a gym or sauna, something that would help riders peel off a few pounds. But it was hard to see past the glaring lights in front of them.

Her foot brushed against the gun and she had another wave of dismay. Being caught with a fake ID was one thing. Entering with an unregistered stolen gun would cause much more of a commotion. But Ana was already inching forward. It was too late to get rid of the weapon.

"Do they use metal detectors here?" she asked, shoving the Glock further beneath the seat and then covering it with an empty sandwich wrapper.

"They use them on the grandstand side," Ana said. "For the public. But I've never seen anyone check the vehicles. So there's no need to worry about that gun."

Nikki exhaled. At least they had that going for them. "Just remember to call me Gloria," she murmured.

A tall dark-skinned man dressed in a crisp khaki uniform waved them forward. Ana lowered her window and passed over a bundle of papers.

He scrutinized the licenses and papers, asked about a Coggins test then walked back and peered into the trailer at Chico. It was only a cursory check and he was back by Ana's window in seconds.

"Okay," he said. But his eyes narrowed on Jorge sitting in the back seat. "Were you in a fight recently?"

Jorge shook his head. "Horse bumped me in the face when we were loading."

"I see," the guard said. But he pulled out the flashlight on his hip and peered into the back. His impassive expression turned to a frown when he spotted Gunner. "Dogs aren't allowed on the grounds," he said. "Only service dogs."

Damn. Nikki wished the guard wasn't so tall. A shorter person might not have noticed Gunner. She leaned toward Ana's lowered window. "He is my service dog," she said.

"What task is he trained to perform?"

She hesitated. The fact that Gunner had been trained for police service wouldn't gain him entry. Security here was privately contracted.

"What service does he provide?" the guard asked, his voice turning crisp.

"Emotional."

"Do you have a current ESA letter?"

"Yes, but not with me." She beamed the man her most apologetic smile. "I can have it delivered tomorrow."

"Sorry," he said. "The dog can't go in with you. There's a boarding kennel two miles down the road."

He pulled a sheet from his clipboard and passed it to Ana. "All the information is there. Just turn around and keep to the right. You'll spot it."

Nikki jerked further over the gear shift, fighting her rush of panic. "But I need him. He's with me all the time."

"You can show us your letter tomorrow."

"But that won't help for tonight!"

The guard studied her for a moment, obviously deciding her agitation was genuine. Which it was. He lowered his clipboard, revealing a glint of empathy in his eyes.

"Just a moment," he said. "I'll check with my boss."

He spoke on his radio to someone called Rick then stepped back to the truck.

"All right," he said, bending down so he could look at Nikki. "But you'll have to drop by the security office tomorrow and show us your letter. And your dog needs to be leashed at all times."

"Thank you." Nikki and Ana both spoke at the same time.

Moments later the gate lifted and they drove onto the grounds, the cab swelled with their collective sigh of relief.

"We did it!" Ana pumped her fist in the air. "And Chico will be more relaxed having Gunner for company. You were good at talking your way in. Is he really a service dog?"

"He's always in service," Nikki said. "I don't know what I'd do without him."

She prayed she'd never have to find out.

CHAPTER TEN

The grounds on the backside of the track were more impressive than Nikki anticipated. Roads curved in several directions, marked by signs pointing to the clubhouse, paddock and barns. A crusher dust walkway, restricted to horse traffic, was deserted at this time of night, but still well lit. There was no Escalade behind them so whoever had been following probably couldn't get past the security gate. She relaxed against the seat, savoring the moment. Chico had made it to his race, safe and sound.

They drove toward the stable area where long narrow barns stretched in rows. A few horses poked their heads over stall doors, watching sleepily as they rolled past. Nikki reached over the seat and patted Gunner, grateful he hadn't growled at the guard so close to Ana's window. It was doubtful he'd have been permitted entry—support dog or not—if he'd shown any sort of aggression. But Gunner was totally chill. Jorge had invited him back up on the seat and he stared out the side window, ears pricked, seeming to regard this as a grand adventure.

The backside was a unique spot, crammed with horse paths, hot walkers and earthy smells. Hanging flower pots gave splashes of color while picnic tables and hammocks added a country feel. A white goat nibbled on a patch of grass, his coat gleaming beneath the barn light.

"Strange that goats can be loose while dogs have to be tied," Nikki said, remembering how the goat at the stable where she and her sister had taken lessons had become a major nuisance. The owners had quietly found it another home.

"Goats are safer," Ana said, barely glancing sideways. "They don't scare the horses. And they eat the same food so they're convenient. Some horses get upset without a companion. A goat is small and can travel with them."

"Is that where the expression 'he got his goat' came from?"

"Maybe. Stealing a goat was the old-fashioned way of upsetting a competitor's horse."

Durant would go a lot further than kidnapping a goat, Nikki thought. But it was reassuring how the barn area was large and well lit. Chico was now just one horse among hundreds. He was safe; her job was done. And the last of her tension drained away.

"Let's get a stall in that shedrow." She gestured at a welcoming barn on her right. A double-wide hammock stretched between two trees, flanked by several wooden chairs. There was grass for Chico to nibble and also dorms close by, which meant convenient shower facilities.

"We're not allowed," Ana said, barely glancing sideways. "Those stalls are for the big trainers, the ones who stay here all year. That's why they're fixed up like that. Ship-ins use the shedrows further from the track. That's where the Durant horses always go."

"Does that mean Durant's men have credentials? They can get in here without a horse?"

"Yes."

Nikki squeezed her eyes shut, suddenly not quite as relaxed. No wonder Durant hadn't tried anything risky on the road. He had the luxury of biding his time. "So Durant knows exactly where we're going?"

"Well, I suppose," Ana said. "Because Chico has an assigned stall, the third one in the shedrow. But I'll be with him every minute, night and day, until the saddle goes on his back. After that, his jockey will take care of him. Chico's jockey is one of the top ten riders here."

"Do you know him well? Your jockey?"

"Not personally. But he's ridden Chico eight times before."

Nikki stared straight ahead, loath to voice her fears. However, Durant had already taken extreme steps to stop Chico from racing. He had men and money, and sadly almost everyone had a price.

"You're certain," she said carefully, "that your jockey can't be influenced?"

"Absolutely. Durant tried to bribe Gary before. Told him to throw a race. But Gary rides to win, every time. Chico is in safe hands."

Nikki rubbed her forehead. Perhaps money wouldn't sway Gary, but there were other ways to influence. And some offers were difficult to refuse. "Does he live on the backside?" she asked.

"No, he owns a house off track. He rides for several big stables so doesn't have to depend on Durant's ship-ins. And Gary has no wives or daughters to rape."

Ana spoke calmly, considering the assaults she'd endured. Amazingly, she didn't want justice; she only wanted Chico. And it was comforting to know the jockey would give Chico a fair shake.

She eased the truck and trailer to a stop by a darkened shedrow at the rear of the grounds. Nikki glanced around, hoping to spot a hammock. No doubt Ana would sleep with Chico, but there wouldn't be any extra floor space in his stall.

However, the truck's headlights revealed a barn very different from the welcoming shedrows they'd passed. There were no chairs or flower baskets or even a grazing goat. There were also fewer horses in residence, judging by the absence of heads peering over stall doors. It reminded her of a one-star motel that catered to budget travelers.

Ana seemed content though and was already reaching for her door handle. "We need to get Chico's stall ready before we unload him," she said. "Water, hay, bedding. But I want to check it out first."

"Doesn't the track maintain the stalls?"

"Yes, but I want to look for any problems. Like sharp nails, loose boards, or moldy hay that could cause colic." Her voice thickened. "I also worry about poison."

Nikki shook her head in disgust. Durant was certainly a snake. There didn't seem to be any limit to his nastiness. "I'll have Gunner give it a sniff," she said.

She pushed open the passenger door and signaled at Gunner. He scrambled over Jorge and leaped to the ground then waited as she clipped on his leash.

She waited a moment, scanning their surroundings, letting her eyes grow accustomed to the dark. She couldn't see much beyond the shedrow but there were no other vehicles on the road and the only sounds came from a whinnying horse.

"Vehicles have to be parked away from the barns," Ana said. "So it's hard to tell if Mr. Durant was here. But I think Chico is safe now."

She trudged toward the stall, her shoulders hunched. She might pretend she was no longer worried but her body language spoke differently.

No one should have to live with fear like that, Nikki thought, striding after her. The idea of poison was appalling. Gunner wouldn't eat anything without permission but Chico was vulnerable. It emphasized how careful they'd have to be with his food and water.

Ana slid the stall door open, the sound jarring in the silence. Seconds later, she jumped back, so violently she almost tripped over Gunner. He cocked his head and stared in the stall, as if wondering why she was upset.

Nikki edged into the stall, comforted by Gunner's reaction, or lack of it. No one was hiding in the corner, waiting to attack. It looked totally normal...except for a white object dangling by a rope hung from the rafters.

She pulled out her phone, using the light to identify it.

"A horse skull," Ana whispered.

Nikki swept her light up and down, revealing a bony ridge on a narrow forehead and huge gaping eye sockets. Unlike a cow skull, it had both upper and lower incisors. Thankfully not human, but Durant's message was clear. Chico was in danger.

Ana pulled a jackknife from her pocket, but her hands were trembling so much she couldn't push the blade through the nylon rope.

Nikki eased the knife from Ana's stiff fingers. "Let me cut it," she said. "I'm a bit taller."

She sliced the rope, relieved the skull wasn't fresh. Unlike the arm in the field, it had no tissue. In fact, when she lowered it to the floor, Gunner barely gave it a cursory sniff.

"Take it to the dumpster," Ana said. "I don't want anyone else to see it."

"Best to keep it so we can show it to authorities."

"No!" Ana made the sign of the cross. "I don't want it anywhere near Chico, or any other horse. It's bad luck. Get it out of here. *Por favor!*"

Nikki moved the skull outside the door. Ana was visibly affected, more upset about an old horse skull than a human arm. Maybe because it was a threat to her beloved horse. However, it went against Nikki's training to dispose of evidence. She rechecked her phone battery. However, it was too low to take a photo.

"I don't want security asking questions," Ana said, her voice strengthening. "They don't like trouble here. Please. Throw it in the dumpster."

Nikki gave a reluctant nod.

"You promise? You'll get rid of it?"

"Yes, I promise."

"Okay. Then I'll help Jorge bring in the straw and hay."

"We better check that Durant didn't leave anything else," Nikki said. The skull might be a diversion, designed to fluster Ana. Clearly it had worked.

She turned a slow circle. The stall lacked the size and opulence of Chico's home accommodations although it appeared safe. The floor consisted of packed dirt, raked clean of old hay and bedding. The walls were empty except for a steel hook hanging close to the door.

Ana pivoted, following Nikki's gaze. "That bucket hook looks sharp. Some people don't worry about things like that. But I'm going to take it out."

She unscrewed the hook, slipped it into her pocket then slid her fingers along several boards. "I'll grab a hammer from the truck and tighten some of these nails," she said. "But otherwise everything is fine."

Gunner seemed similarly content. He sniffed at a few urine stains but otherwise was more interested in staring out the door, checking the trailer where Jorge kept watch over Chico.

"You mentioned poison," Nikki said, sliding the stall door shut so Gunner could concentrate. "What kind are we looking for? Gunner can find a lot of things but he's not trained for that type of search."

"Not technically poison." Ana gave a dismissive shrug, clearly eager to take Chico off the trailer and into the relative comfort of his stall. "A horse's stomach is easily upset. Something as small as a moldy carrot could cause colic. And a nail in the sole of his foot would make him lame. Durant wants to take him out of action, not kill him."

Nikki poked at the hardened dirt with the toe of her shoe. Found nothing sharp or protruding. Certainly there was nothing that would bruise a horse's tender soles. But the skull was too obvious. Durant hadn't followed all this way just to leave a swinging bone.

She unclipped Gunner's leash. "Search."

Without the trailer to distract, Gunner swept around the stall, nose to the ground, checking every corner. He stopped and tilted his head, staring at Nikki, clearly not finding anything he considered worthy.

"Guess it's okay," Nikki said.

Ana wheeled toward the door. "Great. I'll bring in the straw. And screw in a different hook for Chico's water bucket."

"Wait a sec," Nikki said.

Gunner had trotted to the back of the stall, nose in the air. He rose on his hind legs, sniffing against the wall. On two legs, he was almost as tall as a horse. And at a horse's eye level, there was a rounded hole in the board, too perfectly shaped to be a knothole.

He looked over his shoulder at Nikki and then sat, indicating a find.

"Good dog," she said, using a pleased singsong voice.

Gunner's tail thumped the ground, his lip curling in a happy smile.

Ana rushed to the back wall. Balancing on her toes, she pulled out her pocket knife and poked at the hole.

"A piece of apple," she muttered, extracting it with the tip of her knife. "Damn Durant."

"Think it's doctored?"

Ana gave the apple a suspicious sniff. "Probably contains something illegal. Racing is closely monitored and horses are tested after each race. Something as simple as caffeine will show up. Durant knows Chico loves apples. He'd eat it, even if it smells a bit different."

She gave Gunner a grateful pat. "You did well to find this. Now we know everything is safe."

Ana looked relieved but Nikki couldn't help scanning the surrounding darkness. Chico still had to get through the night and it was troubling that Durant knew the location of his stall. Especially one that was so isolated.

"I'll grab a blanket and sleep in the aisle outside Chico's stall," she said. "So Gunner and I will be close by."

"The truck and trailer would be more comfortable," Ana said. "But I'm glad you'll stay with me tonight. Thank you."

"No problem." Nikki found it remarkable that Ana was so gracious and not seething at Durant's attempt to hurt her horse. She wouldn't be nearly as forgiving.

"I know this wasn't how you planned to spend your time," Ana went on. "I'm sorry we wrecked your vacation."

Nikki slid open the stall door, letting Gunner trot back toward the trailer. His tail was high, there was a bounce in his step and he hadn't looked so proud since his gunshot wound. Clearly he relished having a job and thought guarding Chico was much more fun than jogging through the lonely woods. She was having quite a bit of fun too.

"No need to apologize," she said, smiling over her shoulder at Ana. "Our vacation wasn't wrecked. Not one bit."

CHAPTER ELEVEN

An owl hooted, the eerie sound almost drowned out by the deep snores escaping from Chico's stall.

Nikki rose and peered over the stall door, amazed that a tiny person like Ana could make so much noise. It didn't bother Chico. The horse was stretched out in the thick straw, eyes closed, his head only inches from Ana's open mouth.

Maybe he was used to the sound. Perhaps he found it comforting. It was obvious there was a true bond between the woman and her horse.

Not her horse yet. Nikki returned to her watchful position in the aisle, lay down and adjusted the blanket. Gunner gave her cheek a quick lick before putting his head back on his paws and letting out a satisfied groan.

"You like hanging out with horses, don't you," she murmured, inching closer to his warm body.

Jogging clothes weren't great for cool California nights and it would have been more comfortable to sleep in the truck. However, the parking lot was outside the gates and it would be risky to leave Chico alone.

Ana was a determined woman but as the race edged closer, it seemed likely Durant would turn increasingly desperate. He knew Chico's location and was probably aware that his scheme with the apple hadn't worked. The man had all the signs of a sociopath and had proved to be both cruel and cunning.

It was sickening how he'd been terrorizing vulnerable employees. Fortunately Nikki had a picture of the severed arm, and that might be enough to start an investigation. Although the fact that he had control over the local police could be problematic.

Sighing, she rolled over on her back, staring out at the dark sky. Clouds had moved in, blocking the stars. Two stalls down, a horse circled in the straw, also restless. Unlike Chico, he'd been pacing all night.

She shifted onto her hip, searching for the softest spot. The straw bed was okay and she'd certainly slept in worse places. But like the pacing horse, she was too edgy to fall asleep.

According to Ana, the other horses' grooms would arrive at about four-thirty; activity started early at the track. It was already after midnight. So if Durant tried to hurt Chico it would likely be in the next three hours. Would he come or wouldn't he? Ana was sleeping soundly so she must think it was safe. Or maybe she was reassured, knowing Gunner would warn of any intruders.

Nikki peered sideways, checking her dog. His nose was on his paws, his breath slow and easy. But even as she watched, he raised his head, ears pricking.

She peered toward the adjoining shedrow, trying to see what had caught his attention. Saw nothing but yawning blackness. Even the moon had disappeared, wiped out by the clouds. She turned her attention back to Gunner, waiting for him to close his eyes. But he remained riveted on something hidden in the dark.

A growl rumbled deep in his throat.

She tapped his muzzle with a warning finger and reached beneath the blanket, her hand sliding around the Glock.

Gunner stared into the dark, his body taut while Ana continued her blissful snoring. Further along the aisle, a horse played with his water bucket, slurping water like a child. The same sounds they'd been hearing all night, nothing out of the ordinary.

But Gunner was rarely wrong. And he remained rigid, ears pointed toward something in the thick darkness.

Minutes dragged by. She lay unmoving, feeling the pounding of her heart. The adrenaline rush was welcome; she'd been tired waiting for something to happen.

It felt like another ten minutes before a figure finally emerged from the gloom. A man, moving furtively, not pausing by any of the stalls. Moving as if he knew exactly where he was going.

Every few feet, he'd stop and listen. He gripped something in his left hand and wore white running shoes, a poor choice for night work. The man was even smaller than Jorge and didn't resemble any of Durant's muscled goons.

She blew out a relieved breath. This guy was an amateur. She and Gunner would have no problem handling him. She tightened her grip on the gun, preparing to jump from beneath the blanket. Beside her, Gunner quivered with eagerness but held his position.

She studied the creeping man, trying to see what he held in his hand. A gun would cause the most problem. However, the shape was too bulky, almost square. So not a knife, not a gun. Game on.

She waited with bated breath, and a growing degree of impatience. This was the most cautious intruder she'd ever encountered. He tiptoed as if terrified, glancing around at every step. At this speed it would be another two minutes before he reached Chico's stall.

She had to be patient though. Needed to catch him, not scare him away. Wanted to hear him confess he was working for Durant.

Maybe he could even shed some light on the arm Gunner had found.

The restless horse down the aisle abruptly jammed his head over the door. The man leaped and she jerked in automatic reflex. He caught her movement and froze. Then tossed something in the aisle, turned and bolted.

Kicking aside the blanket, she scrambled to her feet, keeping hold of Gunner's collar. She ran down the aisle, slowing slightly to see what the man had dropped.

It was bloody but not a weapon. Only a piece of meat. Obviously intended for Gunner. Just as obviously not a healthy snack.

One of the many lessons Gunner had learned before flunking out of K9 school was never to eat without permission. But her anger spiked, knowing this guy had come to kill her dog.

"Get him," she said, releasing her grip on Gunner's collar.

She charged after them, chasing the spineless coward.

The man was fast. His feet churned in the gravel, white sneakers flashing like pistons. But Gunner closed quickly. Her legs pumped faster and she strained to catch up, glad now she wore her jogging clothes. She didn't want Gunner to get too far ahead just in case the asshole had a hidden knife.

Gunner was growling, his streaking coat camouflaged by the night. But his growls turned to frustrated barks as two white dots danced above his head, high out of reach. Weird. It looked like the man was airborne.

She was running so fast she almost planted her face against the steel mesh of a perimeter fence, camouflaged by the darkness.

Cursing, she jammed the Glock into the back of her waistband and scrabbled up. Originally three strands of razor wire had protected the top. But the wire had been cut, the spot marked by a piece of tape. Clearly the man in the sneakers had planned his getaway, right down to the exact spot for his climb.

She wasn't going to let him escape. If he'd admit he was working for Durant, she could call the police. They wouldn't need Ana's testimony. Poisoning a dog was a felony. So was trespassing.

She scrambled to the top of the rattling fence, carefully angled her body through the cut in the wire and leaped to the ground on the other side, breathless but pumped by the chase. The guy wasn't that far ahead. She'd been faster scaling the fence. Or else the weasel was tiring.

His white sneakers flashed like a beacon. Another twenty strides and she'd catch him. Gunner was barking furiously, stuck on the other side of the fence, but she lowered her head and stubbornly kept running.

Wham. Something smashed into her chest, driving the air from her lungs and knocking her sideways.

"Bitch," a man said, dragging her to her feet. He yanked her hands behind her back. The gun was pulled from her waistband and rough hands ran over her legs, her ass, her breasts.

She couldn't move, couldn't breathe, could only gasp for breath. But she felt the bite of the thin plastic when they tied her hands, the chill of the air on her suddenly bare butt.

"Get her shorts off, all the way. Spread her legs."

Durant. She recognized his voice even though he was talking low. Panic galvanized her. She gave a desperate kick. Her foot landed but someone laughed and grabbed her leg.

"This one's a fighter," a voice growled. A meaty hand clamped over her mouth, his breath thick and hot against her neck. "We're going to want a bit more time with this one, boss. She's got some spice."

"Someone go and shut up that dog," Durant said. His belt buckle clinked.

She wrenched her leg loose and gave another frantic kick. A man grunted in pain. The hand shifted on her mouth and she twisted, trying to tell Gunner to run, but a blow to her head knocked the words from her throat.

She was flung to the ground, spread eagled against the coarse grass. She stared up, her vision spinning. It looked like three men. No, four. She heard the sound of zippers as three men bickered over who would go second and who had to go and shoot the dog.

Behind her, knees pressed against her shoulders, pinning her to the ground. Another man gripped her ankles, yanking her legs wide. Then kneeled between her thighs. The smoky cologne was familiar. And nobody questioned his right to go first. It had to be Durant.

His face was blurry but the voice was clear. "Scratch the horse by seven," Durant said, his voice almost conversational as he insolently squeezed her breast. "Or we'll be the last men to fuck you."

"Someone go and shut that dog up," he ordered, his breath quickening.

She twisted. "Run Gunner!"

Durant clamped his hand over her mouth, snickering when she tried to bite him. "You have bigger worries than your dog."

"Dammit, boss," the man pinning her shoulders said. "We got company."

Her vision was hazy but she could see Gunner's outline as he raged against the fence. Headlights cut the darkness behind him, along with the rumble of a powerful engine.

Durant pressed his mouth close to her ear. "You say anything," he whispered, "and you won't be alive long enough to watch Chico lose. I'll hide you with the horses."

"Fuck you—"

A boot slammed into her ribs, cutting off her curse. And the asshole, either by luck or design, had found almost the exact same place they'd hit her earlier.

She curled in a ball, watching them fade into the gloom, trying to memorize their size and shape. Durant was in the back. The arrogant bastard was barely running, as if he knew they wouldn't be caught. The second guy reminded her of the guard who'd vaulted the fence back at the Durant farm. But her vision didn't feel normal, and she gave her head a shake, struggling to clear it.

When she looked again, there were four shadows, not three. But they were getting smaller, definitely leaving. She squeezed her eyes in relief then shifted and studied her savior's lights.

A dark form was scaling the fence, the rattling mesh protesting under his weight. He must be a good-sized man. Surprisingly Gunner hadn't tried to stop him. And his barking didn't sound as frantic, so maybe he sensed this person was an ally.

"It's okay, Gunner," she said, but her voice was so weak she wasn't sure if he heard.

A man paused by her side then disappeared into the shadows, so quickly Nikki thought she might be hallucinating. But no, Durant and his men wouldn't have left without a reason. And something was parked on the other side of the fence. Looked like a motorcycle. As long as it wasn't an Escalade, she was happy. It meant there truly was a rescuer.

She drew in a shaky breath and sat up. Her arms were tied behind her back and she twisted her wrists, left and right, trying to free them. But the zip ties had been yanked tight. Clearly Durant's men had trussed up women before. Little wonder Ana flinched whenever she mentioned the men.

A wave of nausea swept her and she threw up, unable to control the spasms in her throat.

Gunner's cries sounded pitiful now and she turned her head toward the fence, hoping to reassure him. "It's okay, boy," she managed.

And then the man was back. He kneeled behind her, his hands slow and gentle. "I heard the barking. I'm Rick Talbot, track security. Where do you hurt?"

"Just my pride. You came in the nick of time."

His fingers stilled, as if surprised by her calmness. Seconds later he'd cut the plastic and her hands were free.

She stumbled to her feet, relieved he didn't try to pull her up. She couldn't have accepted a man's touch now, even the hand of a helpful savior. He seemed to understand and remained well back, even turning away and giving her lots of time to gather her shorts and undies.

She pulled them on with trembling hands, furious at herself. Durant had sent a rabbit. Used a fence to immobilize Gunner. And she'd fallen for his trap.

"Are you injured?" Rick asked. "Do you need medical attention?"

"No. I'm not hurt. Like I said, you arrived just in time."

"Then are you able to answer a few questions?" he asked, turning around and studying her.

She stepped back, suddenly wary. He drove a powerful motorcycle, moved like a ninja and even with her blurry vision, she could see the intimidating arm tattoos. Looked like prison ink. And he lacked the khaki uniform that the other track guard wore.

On the other hand, he couldn't be working for Durant or her ambushers wouldn't have run. The guard at the gate had referred to someone named Rick. So the man must be legit. And though Rick's voice was gentle it had a steely core, suggesting he held a position of authority. Probably not the type to overlook attempted rape...which wasn't convenient, considering that she had driven in with Ana. And used a fake ID.

Ana was Chico's trainer on record and couldn't afford a suspension, no matter how short. Chico needed to race tomorrow.

"I don't know those men," Nikki said, her words rushing out. "Chased them without thinking. Guess they were trying to steal our tack."

"So you scaled a wire fence, pursuing a gang of thieves? A woman alone?" His skeptical eyes narrowed over her jogging clothes. "What's your name? I assume you have creds?"

She tugged her shirt further over her hips, struggling to remember the name she'd used. Usually she had an excellent memory but now she could only picture the face on the groom's pass. She crossed her arms and realized she was shaking.

He noticed too, and his voice softened. "You need to warm up."

"Yes, I'd love a hot shower."

"Are you sure they didn't hurt you?"

She knew what he was asking and she gave a curt nod. "Yes. And thank you for stopping those punks. I really want a shower though. Can we talk about this tomorrow?"

He studied her for a long moment. She wiped at her eyes and added a little sniff. He'd already shown his empathy and she needed to take full advantage. Hopefully by the time she ran into him again, Chico's race would be over. And the fact that she'd used fake credentials would no longer matter.

"By the way," she added, the name suddenly popping into her sluggish brain. "My name is Gloria. Gloria Cortes."

"Okay, Gloria. Just one important question for now."

Her heart sunk. Maybe she'd provided the name too triumphantly. He was looking at her oddly, as if he knew she was lying. Judging by the steel in his tone, he didn't intend to let her slip away.

She composed her expression while desperately trying to figure out how to best protect Ana. How to keep any blowback from affecting Chico. "Of course, Rick," she said. "What would you like to know?"

He gave a sudden grin, the smile so disarming it felt out of place in the seedy darkness. But it was his question that really knocked her off balance.

"Why isn't your dog on a leash?" he asked.

CHAPTER TWELVE

Rick Talbot was head of security, drove a motorcycle and seemed utterly committed to keeping the track safe. Whether the danger came from dogs, thieves or trespassers. He was also very much a family man, obvious by the way his voice softened when he called home and explained he'd be working late. He had a wry sense of humor too, reassuring his wife that nothing was wrong and he was just checking out a loose dog.

While he was busy with his call, Nikki retraced her steps along the shedrow, scooped up the dropped piece of meat and jammed it into a garbage container. No doubt it had been poisoned and she didn't want any unsuspecting critter to wander along and eat it. She also didn't want to explain its presence. At least not until she'd talked to Ana.

Rick finished his call and focused his attention back on Nikki. "Go have a shower," he said, gesturing at the concrete building only a stone's throw away. "I'll watch your *tack* until you get back. Then we can discuss what happened."

The idea of a cleansing shower was appealing, but his emphasis on the word "tack" showed he wasn't buying her story that the attackers were random thieves. At least the delay would give her time to think. Ideally she'd like to put off further discussion until after Chico's race.

However, she gave an agreeable nod and hurried toward the shower block with Gunner by her side.

Thankfully the building was empty although the air was still thick with humidity and the scent of herbal soap. She stripped off her clothes and stepped into the tiled stall. The water was hot and welcome, and she tilted her head beneath the powerful spray, relieved a soap dispenser was attached to the wall.

She scrubbed every inch of her skin, determined to erase the memory of those brutal hands. But the harder she rubbed, the more her thoughts pin-balled. Now that she was alone, and safe, she could admit she'd been lucky. Durant had set a trap and she'd literally run into it. It also proved that he was crafty as well as ruthless. No wonder his employees didn't want to face him in court.

Her legs felt buttery soft and she had to steady herself against the wall. The sight of Gunner's nose, poked close to the bottom of the door, was comforting. He always seemed to know when she was unbalanced.

Straightening, she remained beneath the steaming water for long minutes, hoping to cleanse her body and emotions, reluctant to leave its warm refuge. She was even more reluctant to pull on her dirty clothes, clothes that Durant had touched.

Finally she turned off the faucet and stepped out, gathering some paper towels and drying herself as much as possible. Then she wiped the condensation from the mirror. The face staring back appeared haunted, with eyes too big against her ashen face. But at least her vision had returned to normal. She twisted, checking the marks on her shoulders. Already bruises had formed.

When she tugged her clothes back on, goose bumps rose over her skin and it wasn't because of the thin fabric. In fact, she was even more chilled after dressing, as if Durant and his men were touching her again.

It was tempting to dump her clothes in the garbage, and she checked every corner of the shower block, searching for castoffs. Found nothing except a wet washcloth and two mismatched socks. The horse blanket would have been useful but she hadn't thought to bring it. Had been in too much of a hurry to wash away the ugliness. Clearly it wasn't going to be as simple as taking a hot shower.

She slammed the door shut and strode from the shower block with an anxious Gunner close to her side.

"It's okay. They're gone," she said, talking as much to herself as to him. But she froze at the sight of a flickering phone screen, ominously close to Chico's stall. And now she had no gun. Seconds later she realized it was only Rick, seated on a hay bale.

Her heart steadied. Durant and his men were long gone. Certainly Ana and Chico couldn't have had any better protection while she was in the shower. But her hand searched for Gunner's head, needing his solid presence.

Rick rose politely, waiting until she'd sat down. But his eyes narrowed over her jogging clothes. "Don't you have anything warmer to wear?"

"We left the stable in a hurry," she muttered, scooping up the horse blanket and draping it over her shoulders. "No time to pack."

"Want to call someone? Arrange for suitable clothes? Or maybe just to talk?"

She shook her head. She didn't want to talk; didn't want to think about the attack. Right now, she felt too fragile. And that bothered her. PI's were supposed to be tough.

"What I really want is an iPhone charger," she said, trying for a lighter tone. "And some sleep."

She leaned back on her makeshift bed, determined to postpone any more of his questions. She was too wired to think properly although getting any sleep was wildly optimistic. It was impossible to forget Durant: his words, his touch, her horrible helplessness. She was used to helping victims, not being one. And her experience wasn't even comparable to what Ana had endured. Time and time again.

"I just need to clarify a few things," Rick said, his eyes dipping back to his phone. "I see you're employed with the Durant stable. Our records show that you and Ana Gonzalez came in with Durant's horse, Chico's Kid. Along with an exercise rider, Jorge Diaz."

"That's right," she said. "We arrived about five hours ago."

"Where are Jorge and Ana now?"

"Jorge is sleeping in the trailer. And Ana is sleeping in Chico's stall." She gestured toward the stall and the sound of snoring.

Rick gave a glimmer of a smile but continued his questions. "You've never brought a dog before, Gloria," he said. "And this is private property. If he poses a direct threat to the safety of others, he can't stay. You stated at the security gate that he was an emotional support dog?"

"Yes, for PTSD," she murmured, her gaze flickering to Rick's phone. He was obviously able to access the guard's log, including the fact that she'd checked in as Gloria Cortes. Generally she had no problem using different identities. In her line of work, it was a job requirement. But she couldn't jeopardize Ana's standing at the track and clearly Rick wasn't the type to condone the use of false credentials.

She jerked forward, her thoughts still on Durant. And how the guard's log might help nail him. "Can you see all the people who came in tonight? Is David Durant's name there? Or any of his men?"

"This will go much faster," Rick said, "if I ask the questions."

She pressed her lips together but her mind whirled. If she could prove Durant had entered the backside, maybe he could be charged with attempted rape. Ana wouldn't have to be involved.

But Rick leaned forward. "So you *do* know the men who attacked you?"

She fiddled with the blanket, adjusting it higher around her neck, wishing Ana was awake so they could discuss this. But Ana had made it clear she didn't want any part of a court case. And Nikki had accepted that...until the encounter tonight. However, Durant had made it personal.

"If you know who attacked you," Rick went on, "just give me their names. Everyone has the right to feel safe. If it includes Durant, I'll have him suspended, along with any horses he owns."

She gulped. That would be the worst course of action. Chico had to run tomorrow. Clearly Rick wasn't the type to brush off an assault and usually she would find his quick support admirable. But not here. Not now.

"Help me do my job," Rick said. "You chased four men over an eight-foot fence. Why?"

"I thought there was only one guy," she said, trying to make a joke.

"You didn't bring clothes suitable for the track," Rick said, not smiling. If anything his expression turned more serious. "Are you really a groom?"

She nodded, relieved he hadn't asked if she really was Gloria Cortes. But this man was too concerned about rules. A Dudley do-gooder. She had to give him something. And elements of the truth were always better than outright lies.

"We left in a hurry," she said, choosing her words carefully. "Ana has a contract that if Chico wins one more race, she'll own him. So she didn't want anything to happen, like a truck breakdown or something that might cause him to miss the race...or be suspended."

Rick tilted his head, staring in silence. Seconds dragged but Nikki knew all the interrogation tools and simply waited him out.

"So Durant owns the horse?" Rick finally said. "But only if the animal never wins again? So he may not want the horse to run?"

"Exactly." She put a hand over her mouth, faking a yawn, guessing that Rick was too kind to put her through any more questions tonight.

But he continued to scroll over his phone, studying data only he could see. Light from the screen spotlighted his stubborn jaw and despite his empathy, it drove home the fact that he wasn't the type to brush off criminal assaults. "What's the horse's registered name?" he asked.

She rolled her neck, stalling for time. As the horse's groom, she should definitely know Chico's full name. But her mind was blank.

She opened and closed the snap on the blanket, playing it between her fingers, and the routine action calmed her brain, restoring her usually excellent memory. Now she could even picture the sign on the horse's stall, the beautiful brass letters on the expensive wood.

"His registered name is Chico's Kid," she said. "But around the barn we call him Chico."

"Doesn't seem likely that he'll win tomorrow," Rick said. "It's been a while since he won a graded stakes. The track handicapper has him at forty to one."

"Durant picked a tough race on purpose."

"So we agree Chico's a longshot," Rick said, still staring at the screen. "And Ana is desperate to win, and perhaps Durant is just as desperate that Chico doesn't. As a result, we have thugs lurking around the track." He shot Nikki a quizzical look. "And you claim to be a groom. Even though you're dressed for a track meet."

He abruptly lifted his phone and snapped a picture of her and Gunner.

"Hey. You need my permission for that."

His eyes narrowed and she stopped protesting.

"Look," he said, his voice gentle. "I don't like a lot of drama. It would be safer for everyone if Ana scratches the horse. He's not likely to win anyway. She's welcome to come back after this is sorted out. And I'll help you talk to the police about what happened tonight."

"But Durant is retiring Chico. This is her last chance to reach twenty wins."

"So he hired a bunch of goons to stop him. And he's getting desperate. Which is exactly why it's not safe for the horse to be here." Rick gestured at Gunner. "And your dog doesn't look like a typical support animal, not the way he wanted to eat those men. Dogs like that shouldn't be near a public track. If they get riled, they're hard to control. I have backstretch workers along with race fans to protect. People who pay good money so they can cheer and shout and wave their arms. That type of behavior can worry a dog."

Nikki kept her face impassive but there was a lot of truth to his words. He seemed to understand dogs.

"An indiscriminate bite would be a PR nightmare," Rick went on. "You certainly didn't run from trouble tonight. In actuality, you were running toward it. So be honest with me, Gloria, what is your real role with Ana?"

She gave a long sigh, trying to sound more aggrieved than worried. She didn't want to provide any more ammunition for scratching the horse. Besides, if Rick was working tonight, he'd be sleeping most of tomorrow. By the time he came back to write up a formal report, Chico's race would be over.

"I'm just a groom," she said. "A very tired one."

"Before you go to sleep, I'd like to see your creds."

"Sure, but everything is locked away. After we pulled them out at the gate we left them in Ana's truck."

He scowled. "They need to be with you at all times. And speaking of Ana, that's another concern. I hate to think you're taking advantage of her situation. Maybe charging her for some sort of security service?"

"Absolutely not!" Nikki's fingers curled into her hands, stung by his inference.

"It happens. Workers are abused, offered sweetheart deals that are never paid, yet they're afraid to ask authorities for help. Too worried about deportation. They end up wasting money they don't have, for services they never receive."

"Ana's not paying me for protection," she said.

"Good. Because you were the one who needed protection tonight."

She sucked in an achy breath. He was right and the truth hurt. Gunner growled deep in his throat, looking around for whatever was bothering her.

"You need to understand that the safety of everyone here is my concern," Rick went on. "That's the intent behind the rules. The track isn't the place to settle disputes."

"But Chico is here now," she said. "Along with Ana. So their safety is also your concern."

"For now, yes," Rick said. "But this sounds like a police matter. And I don't want a horse that's a magnet for violence."

He must have seen her stiffen because his voice softened. "If you want to pursue this, I'll back you up with the authorities. Tell them what I saw tonight. But for the record, the only Durant employees officially on the backside tonight were you, Ana and Jorge."

Durant was slippery, Nikki thought, shoving back a strand of wet hair. She'd been attacked on the other side of track property. And whoever had messed with Chico's stall had no doubt scaled the fence. It would be hard making anything stick if she couldn't prove he was here. No doubt he and his men would have iron-clad alibis as to their whereabouts tonight.

She slumped back against the straw, rocked with a bone-deep weariness. She just wanted to protect Ana. Needed Rick to go. Didn't want to reveal anything more that might mess up Chico's race.

"Can we talk about this tomorrow?" she asked. "I need to think about Durant and whether I want to file charges. But I really appreciate your help, especially, you know, earlier...." She squeezed the blanket, pushing away the memory of those rough hands.

"Of course," Rick said, rising to his feet. "We'll figure this out. I'm sorry about what happened tonight."

She nodded, feeling a bit guilty about appealing to his empathy. But Ana had endured unspeakable abuse merely to get

Chico to the starting gate. She'd made it clear that security here was quick to step in. So honesty with Rick would have to wait.

"See you tomorrow," Nikki said, tilting on her side so she could face Chico's stall, knowing that despite her exhaustion she wouldn't sleep a wink. Durant was both twisted and stubborn. He might return.

"I'm not leaving," Rick said. "In light of what you told me, I'll stay and watch out for the horse. Try and get some sleep."

She gave a grateful nod. He might be prickly about safety but he seemed to genuinely care about people. Maybe she should admit her real name, along with her occupation. Probably he could be persuaded to bend the rules.

But Rick's voice changed, turning official. "Don't forget to tie your dog," he said. "And tomorrow I want to see your creds."

"Roger that," she said.

CHAPTER THIRTEEN

Nikki was pulled out of a deep sleep by what felt like a warm washcloth rubbing against her cheek.

"Morning, Gunner," she whispered, gently pushing her dog's head away. He obviously thought it was time for her to wake. It was still dark, the air cool and crisp. But already people moved along the shedrow, murmuring greetings and rattling grain buckets. She didn't want to move from beneath the cozy blanket. Surprisingly, she'd slept like a rock, reassured that Rick was keeping watch.

Yawning, she sat up and peered at Chico. He looked bright and happy, chewing hay and staring at Gunner, unaware he was the center of a firestorm. Ana was only fifteen feet away, chatting animatedly with Jorge and a gray-haired woman.

Further down the aisle, grooms rolled out hoses and pushed laden wheelbarrows. The smell of horse and hay was everywhere.

She twisted, checking beyond the shedrow. A khaki-clad security guard, a short man with a bit of a paunch, stood by a nearby lamp pole, obviously Rick's replacement. Which probably meant Rick had gone home to sleep. Hopefully he'd stay away well into the afternoon.

She pushed aside the blanket then gave an involuntary wince. Her ribs ached and both shoulders hurt where Durant's man had held her against the ground. The cold air didn't make her feel any better. She pulled the blanket back up, remaining in a sitting position, reluctant to leave its soothing warmth.

Ana walked over, smiling and looking much more relaxed than she ever had at Durant's stable.

"Good, you're finally awake," she said.

"What time is it?"

"Five-thirty. You slept like a baby. So did Chico. He's feeling great, ready to run." Her smile turned to a frown. "Don't let your dog pee on that hay. We don't have any extra."

Gunner was in the process of lifting his hind leg and Nikki called for him to stop. "Go over there, fellow," she said, gesturing toward a nearby sycamore tree.

The guard immediately hurried over. "That dog can't be loose. He needs to be leashed."

"It's only twenty feet away," Nikki said. "And he's very obedient."

"No exceptions," the guard said. Judging by the set of his shoulders, he was just as stubborn about rules as his boss.

Ana quickly scooped up Gunner's leash and passed it to Nikki. Clearly she didn't want anything messing up Chico's race. At some point, she'd have to be updated on last night's encounter, and how Durant might be charged with assault. For now though, it was apparent she didn't want to think too far ahead. Didn't want to stress about how she and Jorge had no jobs or a place to live. And if Chico didn't win today, she'd have no horse.

Thinking of Ana's predicament only increased Nikki's early-morning crankiness. Security here was so anal, wasting everyone's time obsessing about mundane little rules when there was a sociopath lurking.

"Were you sent here to give out dog tickets?" she snapped.

"No," the guard said. "Boss told me to watch the horse in stall ten. And to give you this."

He reached out, placed a bag on the hay and calmly returned to his vantage point.

She opened the bag, her eyes widening at its contents: a thermos of coffee with three paper cups, a hooded sweatshirt with the track logo, a bottle of pain pills, and a phone charger. There was even a plastic baggie stuffed with what looked to be homemade dog treats.

"Thank you so much," she called. "Sorry I was grouchy. You and your boss are awesome!"

The guard gave a wry salute.

She pulled on the warm fleece, clipped on Gunner's leash and walked him to a nearby tree, relieved to see that his gait was even and he'd suffered no setbacks from last night.

Smiling, she returned to the hay bales, sat down beside Ana and twisted open the thermos.

"This has got to be the best track ever," she said, pouring the hot coffee and passing cups to Ana and Jorge. The coffee was strong and black, the way she'd learned to like it after long hours of surveillance. Just the smell of it jumpstarted her brain, replacing her frustration with a warm contentment.

Jorge seemed to be feeling better too. He took his coffee with an agreeable nod, patted Gunner on the head then joined a circle of men in the adjoining shedrow, moving rather sprightly for someone who'd absorbed several punishing blows less than twenty-four hours earlier.

Ana remained seated, her puzzled gaze on the thermos. "I agree that it's a nice track," she said. "But I've never had coffee delivered before."

"I met the head of security last night," Nikki admitted. "Rick Talbot."

"He keeps tight control," Ana said. "And my friends all trust him to keep everyone safe. That's why we no longer have to worry about Chico. And probably why we slept so well."

Nikki sipped her coffee, debating how much to tell her. Ana and Chico were both relaxed and that was important before a race. There was probably no need to cause her concern. Not yet.

"You're right," Nikki said. "They certainly are keeping close tabs on Gunner."

"But leashing dogs is a good thing," Ana said. "Everyone's livelihood revolves around the track. Horses and people have to be kept safe. That's why we need to follow the rules."

Nikki stifled a smile. Ana seemed to have conveniently forgotten that Nikki was posing as someone else. She was a cool lady, outwardly submissive but inside had the heart of a rebel, especially when it aided Chico. And perhaps there were some other rules that she was breaking.

"You mentioned that one of Durant's threats was deportation," Nikki said. "What about you and Jorge? Do you have valid work permits?"

"Mine is good but Jorge's has expired. And Durant knows. He prefers to hire undocumented workers because we can't go to the police for help."

"Maybe police here would be more understanding. Especially if you told them about the abuse."

Ana gave a forceful shake of her head. "No, then Chico's ownership would be tied up in court for years. And it would be way too expensive. The system doesn't work for us."

She wasn't wrong. Nikki took a pensive sip of coffee, thinking of Justin trying to present evidence that was often challenged. High-powered lawyers made a difference. And Durant would be able to afford the best.

They drank their coffee in silent companionship, tipping the thermos for refills, watching Chico munch his hay. He looked as content as a backyard pet, a dependable horse that a child could trust on a trail ride. His behavior was much different than the Thoroughbreds Justin owned, and that made Nikki worry.

"Truthfully," she said, "does Chico have any chance of winning?"

"I believe in him," Ana said. "He's the oldest horse in the race and there are five horses with faster times. But he doesn't have any quit. And he'll know the race is important."

"How will he know?" she asked.

"Because he knows me. And he'll feel the jockey's urgency. Just like your dog senses it's important to be obedient while the security guard is watching."

Nikki smiled down at Gunner. His nose was stuck an inch from her foot, his eyes locked on Chico. Clearly he wanted to be closer to the horse but he wasn't pulling at his leash. And he hadn't growled or acted aggressive, hadn't worried about the male grooms rushing along the aisle so close to where she sat.

He certainly couldn't be faulted for last night's aggression. Sure, he'd have eaten Durant if he'd had the chance. And she would have let him.

Just the thought of Durant made her jumpy. She stuck her hand in the dog bag and passed Gunner a treat, wishing she could push the man from her head.

"So what's the schedule?" she asked. "What time is Chico's race?"

"It's the eighth race on the card," Ana said. "Chico's jockey is coming in an hour to jog him around the track. Then I'll take him over to the paddock and let him see it. He's more confident when he's familiar with everything. And he likes a routine. After his morning exercise, Jorge and I will give him a bath and let him graze a bit, like I did at the stable.

"We just have to get him to the starting gate," she added. "The jockey will do the rest. So you don't have to worry anymore."

It was impossible to quit worrying though. Nikki couldn't shake the fear that Rick might show up before race eight, demanding to see her non-existent credentials. It wouldn't be such a disaster if she were kicked out but it would be grossly unfair if he penalized Ana. Especially since all this trouble was because of Durant.

She checked the serene road again. Pre-dawn traffic was sparse. A feed truck and a farrier's van chugged past, their lights cutting the darkness, but fortunately there was no telltale rumble of a motorcycle.

"Stop worrying," Ana repeated. "Security won't let Durant hurt Chico. They're quick to kick people out before trouble starts."

"Great," Nikki said, forcing a strained smile.

CHAPTER FOURTEEN

The sun had fully risen, spotlighting the shedrow along with Ana's growing agitation. Now she was the one watching the road. She paced back and forth, checking over her shoulder and wringing her hands.

"It's eight thirty! Gary should have been here by now. Chico is missing his chance to get out on the track."

Nikki gave a troubled nod, knowing she could do little to calm Ana. Chico was saddled and tied in the stall, still waiting for his jockey. Most of the other horses in the shedrow had already returned from their morning gallop and had been bathed and cooled.

Training hours closed soon; gates opened to the public at eleven and Chico's race was at three. It wouldn't be good to keep him cooped up. He needed to stretch his legs. And even though Chico had raced here before, it was always wise to familiarize a horse with his surroundings.

"Maybe Jorge could take him out," Nikki said.

"That would be better than nothing," Ana said. "But Chico needs his jockey. They have to get reacquainted before the race."

"Is Gary usually late?" Nikki asked, wondering if Durant had warned the jockey off but loath to voice her suspicions.

"No, he's usually reliable," Ana muttered, her steps slowing at the sound of an approaching vehicle. "Probably that's him."

A worker rounded the corner, pedaling a bicycle. Then a white Jeep filled the narrow road. Clearly not the jockey, judging by Ana's disappointed sigh. And then Nikki noted the track logo emblazoned on the vehicle door, recognized Rick's face behind the wheel.

He unfolded from the driver's seat, his expression too grim to be bearing good news. He strode past Nikki, his attention on Ana.

"Are you Ana Gonzalez?" he asked. "The trainer on record for Chico's Kid?"

He waited for her nod before continuing. "I'm sorry to advise that Gary Lopez was in a car accident this morning. He's off all his mounts and won't be able to ride your horse."

Ana clutched at her throat, her eyes widening. "He'll be okay?"

"Yes. The airbag saved him. But he'll be in the hospital for a while."

Rick swung around, looking even bigger than he had last night. "Nikki Drake," he said, enunciating her name loud and crisp. "Please come with me."

Nikki swallowed. Damn, he was efficient. Why wasn't he sleeping? And how had he figured out her identity so quickly? Then she remembered the picture he'd snapped with his phone. He must have used a face-matching program.

She peeked at Ana who looked similarly alarmed, obviously noting that he had called Nikki by her real name.

"Tie your dog," Rick said. "And walk to my vehicle. Now." He didn't say "please" again.

She stooped and tied Gunner to the post. "Stay," she said, her thoughts whirling.

Rick remained five steps behind, herding her toward his Jeep. She sensed his eyes boring into her back, could feel his radiating anger. But she held her head high and slid into the passenger's seat before he could direct her to sit in the back.

He folded his big body behind the wheel then leveled her with a look that rivaled Justin's iciest cop glare.

"You lied to me," he said. "About your PI license and your role. Not only that, I learned your dog attacked a groom at the Durant stable. Totally unprovoked. Yet you brought him here. To my track!"

Not his track, she thought. But that wasn't the issue. And she knew she had to stay calm, lay out the facts.

"It wasn't unprovoked," she said. "Gunner was protecting Ana and Jorge. And the man wasn't a groom. He was one of Durant's thugs, part of the same group that attacked me last night."

Rick raised a silencing hand.

"Maybe so," he said. "But the police down there want to talk to you. You can straighten it out with them."

"That won't work, considering they're in Durant's pocket."

"Not my jurisdiction. But using false ID to gain track admission is. You also misrepresented your dog as a support animal. And PTSD isn't a joke. Now tell me, what astronomical fee are you charging Ana?"

"She isn't paying me anything. Like I told you last night, she just needed a little help."

"You told me many things last night, most of which were lies."

"My PTSD is real," Nikki said. "And I do need Gunner for support."

Rick studied her face then gave a curt nod. "I'll give you that. But I still don't believe your *questionable* protection services are free. Or effective. As I recall, you needed my help last night."

His belittling tone made her flush. Yes, she'd needed help last night but she certainly didn't need his snide reminder. Every little detail was seared in her brain: the sound of Durant's belt buckle, the stink of his cologne, her horrifying helplessness.

"There was no fee involved," she said stiffly. "I just wanted to help Ana."

"So she asked for your assistance?"

"No, I was jogging by the Durant property and Gunner found a bone."

"Something like this?" He reached behind the seat, scooped up something and plopped it on her lap.

The horse skull. She jerked away, recoiling at the empty eye sockets staring back at her. Rick must have fished it out of the garbage bin. Clearly the man didn't sleep. And the fact that he was so thorough was unexpected. She'd expect this type of follow-up from a detective like Justin, not from a random security guy at a modest racetrack.

She gathered her composure, accepting he wouldn't be satisfied with anything less than the truth. Best to explain the situation and why it was so important for Chico to race.

"Actually the other bone wasn't like this skull," she said. "In fact it was a human arm, still fleshed and showing traces of lye."

"Did you notify the police?"

"Of course. That's why I was on Durant's property. They told me to meet them there."

"Yet you felt you had to get involved?"

"They weren't prepared to do anything. And Ana was worried Durant would hurt Chico."

"So you assumed the horse was in danger. And that you could handle it better than the police. Or my security."

"Chico *is* in danger. In fact this skull was hanging in his stall when we arrived—a threat your questionable security didn't prevent."

Remorse flickered across his face and she instantly regretted her comment. Security here was excellent. She'd retaliated because of his dig at her competence.

"The fact that we couldn't prevent it is precisely the problem," he said, his clipped speech showing she'd hit a tender spot. "You led this bone trail here. And expect us to keep Ana and the horse safe. On a day when we'll have over five thousand spectators. Not a risk I'm willing to take."

He clamped his hands over the wheel, his voice as tight as his grip. "So you. That horse. And all the stable's connections need to leave. Now."

She slumped in the seat, paralyzed with dismay. She shouldn't have been so honest. And chasing that intruder last night had been a mistake, spurred by anger at what she'd believed was an attempt to poison Gunner. Durant had known how to push her buttons.

"Please let Chico race," she said. "It was my idea to use Gloria's ID and to stay with him on the backside. Ana had nothing to do with it. She won't talk much about the bones or Durant's abuse, but the man's a rapist and I suspect he's also a murderer. She genuinely needed help."

"Your intentions might have been good," Rick said. "But that horse has to go. It's too risky. My security can't handle Durant."

"But he can't be allowed to get away with this."

"I agree," Rick said. "But it's not the track's job."

"So you stake out your local piece of community and keep that safe? You don't care about anyone else?"

"Bingo." He gave a sardonic smile. "My family lives here so I'm doubly motivated to keep out the murderers."

That explained his zealousness. She'd already gathered he was a dedicated family man and genuinely cared about the track community. But that didn't help Ana.

"So you accept Durant is dangerous," she said, frustration barbing her voice. "Yet you're wrecking Ana's chance to own Chico. After all she's endured."

"My sympathies are with any exploited workers. But lives are more important. For everyone's safety, that horse has to go. He can come back and race another time."

That wouldn't happen, she thought bleakly. Durant would make sure Chico was in no shape to run again. It could be a foot problem, cut ligaments, or even a deliberate blinding. Something would happen, something horrible. Durant knew how much Ana loved the horse and would want to cause maximum pain.

"Chico has to race today," she said. "It's their last chance."

"No. The horse is leaving."

His tone didn't leave much room for argument. But Justin had taught her a lot about California racing, and she knew security wasn't in charge of race decisions.

She squared her shoulders. "Then I'll report you to the Race Board," she said. "I wonder what reason you'll give them for suspending Chico."

Rick didn't hesitate. "Presenting false creds. Misrepresenting a service dog. Having a dangerous animal off leash. I could make up more. But there's no need. The Board doesn't question my decisions." This time his smile was genuine, and also infuriating.

"But those infractions are on me! Not Ana. I'll take my dog and go. Just let Chico run."

"I can't have that horse here. Based on what you told me, Durant is dangerous and unpredictable. If it's any consolation, Chico doesn't have much chance of winning. His odds went up even higher after he lost his jockey to a hit and run." Rick's voice hardened. "And his jock, by the way, is a good friend of mine."

"More reason not to let Durant get away with this."

"I didn't say he'd get away with it."

She brightened, alerted by the promise in his voice. "Really? What are you going to do?"

"Gather evidence, turn it over to the proper authorities. Let them stop him."

"What if there's no evidence?"

"I'll find something," he said.

She tilted her head, trying to read his expression, to understand the meaning behind his words. But he was staring straight ahead and she couldn't see his eyes, only his uncompromising jaw. And the knowledge hit her like a sledge hammer. She'd been wrong about him. Rick wasn't a stickler for the rules; he was someone who preferred to make them. And he was happy to bend them—if and when it suited his purpose.

Unfortunately, his purpose today was to keep the track trouble-free.

She slowly set the skull on the floor. There was nothing left to say. Allowing Chico to stay wouldn't further Rick's goal. In his position, she'd probably do the same thing. And maybe he would make life tough for Durant. But that wouldn't be in time to help Ana.

"How long do we have to pack up?" she asked.

"An hour. I'll advise security to let Jorge bring the trailer in so he won't have to wait in line."

"How kind of you," she said. But it wasn't in her nature to give up and she couldn't resist one last appeal. "Can't Chico stay and race? Remember, Durant hurt your friend. Gary could have been killed in that car accident. The best revenge would be if Chico won—"

"We're finished talking." He slapped a business card on the dashboard. "Have Ana call this number. They'll find her and Jorge a safe place to stay. Help them find new jobs."

"Fine," Nikki said, hating the quaver in her voice. "But she'll lose Chico. And that horse means everything to her."

"That's unfortunate. But Gary was blindsided by a truck this morning. You were nearly raped last night. Could have been killed. No one else is going to get hurt over this. Not on my watch. And nothing is changing my mind."

He pushed open the door, his jaw as hard as granite and just as immovable. "Let's go," he said.

She stepped out of the Jeep and trudged toward the shedrow, shooting him dark looks that he completely ignored. And maybe Chico had no realistic chance of winning—especially without his regular jockey—but to deny him the chance of trying was cold-hearted. She rolled and unrolled her fists, working up the courage to tell Ana.

Maybe Rick intended to break the news. He carried an officious pink pad; it looked like the form had already been filled out. Maybe he'd wordlessly pass it to Ana. Or perhaps he'd nail the notice on the stall door. Nikki had no idea of the proper procedure, and she now knew he didn't always care about following it.

She trailed him toward Chico's stall. However, the door was open; both Ana and the horse were gone. And the idea of Rick chasing after a fleet-footed Ana, trying to serve notice, would have made her laugh if the situation weren't so grim. Maybe he wouldn't be able to find her. Ana had proven to have a survivor's sense of when it was wise to hide.

Gunner wasn't at all agitated. He sat where she'd tied him and though he wagged his tail at her approach, his attention returned to a spot on her left. She followed his gaze and quickly spotted Chico.

Ana held the horse by the adjacent shedrow, behind a mechanical hot walker. Chico pawed the ground, saddled and ready to go, unaware his only exercise would be to walk onto the trailer. Ana was talking to a striking dark-haired woman, just as unaware that Rick was about to deliver devastating news.

"Just trot him around once," Ana said loudly as she boosted the petite woman onto Chico's back. "Thanks for coming at such short notice."

"No problem. I'm always happy to ride a quality horse." The woman gave a gracious nod then turned in Nikki's direction and flashed a beautiful smile. A smile with a hint of an apology.

Ana quickly turned Chico and led the horse and rider toward the track.

Nikki felt Rick's stillness, and something else. Consternation. It was then that she understood the rider's expression. The woman hadn't been smiling at Nikki. She'd been looking past her. Toward Rick.

"Who's the rider?" she asked.

"Eve," he said. "My wife."

CHAPTER FIFTEEN

Nikki bounced on her toes, ecstatic about the turn of events. There was no longer any fear of Rick suspending Chico—not when his wife was so keen to ride the horse. Now there were also two security guards posted at each end of Chico's shedrow. And Rick was sticking to their new jockey like a burr. No way would Durant get past him.

Somehow Ana had managed the one possible feat that would allow Chico to stay.

"How did you know?" Nikki asked, shaking her head in admiration.

Ana's smile was deservedly smug. "When Rick used your real name and took you to his Jeep, I knew we were in big trouble. His wife was in the next shedrow so I ran over and asked her to exercise Chico. She promised if they got along, she'd ride him in the race."

Ana thrust a triumphant fist in the air. "And they got along great. Chico floated over the track. Eve is a quiet rider. I know he'll try hard for her."

"I'm so relieved," Nikki said. "I thought I'd messed everything up."

"No way. You helped us escape Durant. And got Chico here, safe and ready to run. Eve said he strutted around the track like a rock star."

Chico looked like he was ready to race. He'd returned from his morning exercise with a glint in his eye and a bounce in his step. Gunner was now tied in front of his stall while Chico tugged at his hay net, dropping stalks of hay and playfully lipping them off the dog's back.

"Is Eve as good as your original jockey?" Nikki asked, rather curious about Rick's beautiful wife with the flashing eyes and confident smile.

"Yes. She doesn't have Gary's experience but probably has more natural talent. She was a jockey on the rise at Santa Anita a while back but doesn't like to ride green horses anymore. Not after her second baby. She took out a training license though and still rides select horses. So she's in good shape."

Nikki nodded. Her first impression of Eve had been that she was petite but every inch an athlete. "Does she know your situation with Chico? Why the race is so important?"

"Yes, that's why she's doing it. She's a big supporter of the track community and started a child care program here. We have some mutual friends who work in the kitchen. She'll do her best to help Chico win. And she's not afraid of Durant. I don't think she's afraid of anything."

Eve certainly knew how to handle her husband. And Rick had a powerful personality. Earlier he'd claimed there was no way he was changing his mind about Chico. Yet Eve had done it without any drama, simply by climbing on the horse.

Admittedly Rick hadn't been pleased. His concern that his wife had stepped into Durant's firing line had been obvious. Nikki wouldn't want Durant plotting against anyone she loved either. There didn't seem to be any limits on what the man might do.

Yet Rick hadn't tried to stop Eve from riding. And he'd said nothing more about banning Chico. Clearly his wife's happiness was paramount, and he wasn't about to interfere with her riding career. Maybe Chico had no real chance of winning but at least he'd be able to compete. Certainly Chico and Eve didn't act like underdogs. They both had a natural swagger.

Durant might be even more worried about the emergence of this more-talented jockey. But if he planned to hurt Chico or Eve, he'd have to do it soon. The race was less than three hours away.

Nikki pivoted, scanning the road, the horse path and the adjacent shedrow, checking for anyone who looked out of place.

"You can stop worrying," Ana said, following her gaze. "Eve is sequestered in the jockeys' room and Chico has track security. I admit he's a longshot. But without you, he never would have made it to the track. And I still have a chance to own him. That was always the intent of the agreement."

Nikki gave a tight smile. That agreement might have been intended to reward loyal workers but it had created misery after Durant Sr. died. And though everyone seemed safe now, she couldn't shake her unease. Chico was worth millions as a stud. Durant would be furious if the horse was shipped to Chile. No doubt he wished Ana would drop dead.

Everyone was focused on protecting Chico and his new jockey. But maybe Ana was the real target. The sloping hill behind the adjacent barn would provide the perfect spot for a shooter. Once Ana left the shedrow, even if it was only to walk to the washrooms, she'd be an easy mark.

"Do you happen to know," Nikki asked, keeping her voice casual, "what would happen if you died before Chico's race?"

Ana gave a satisfied smile. "If my death were within twenty-four hours of Chico's win, my heirs would own the horse. So five o'clock yesterday was the cutoff. Durant will not gain anything by killing me. Not now."

"So that's why you were hiding in Chico's stall yesterday. You must have been terrified. Counting down the hours."

"Yes, too afraid to take Chico for his morning grass. It helped that you reported the bone that Gunner found. Nothing much could happen while the police were around. And then you appeared like a guardian angel. Stopping that guard and getting us here safely." She swallowed, her throat moving convulsively. *"Muchas gracias."*

Nikki squeezed Ana's hand. The gratitude felt good, coming after Rick's scornful dismissal of her skills. "Gunner was a big help," she said. "And we still need Chico to win. Gunner can't help with that."

"No, he can't," Ana said. "But we are here. Just one more win. I've been working a long time for this. Living in fear. Afraid I'd end up buried with the horses."

Nikki tilted forward, locking on Ana's words. Durant had said something similar last night. At the time, she hadn't taken his words literally.

"Are horses buried on the property?" she asked.

Ana shrugged and stared at her feet, as usual not wanting to talk about the threats and abuse—or anything related to Durant. Nikki had always respected that wish. However, the implications of a burial ground were too chilling to ignore.

"You keep referring to what Gunner found yesterday as a bone," she went on. "But it wasn't an old horse skull. It was a human arm. Is it possible Durant buried more than horses?"

Ana wrapped her arms around her chest, still studying the ground.

"Do you really believe the severed arm was from a morgue?" Nikki asked. "Or is that the easy explanation?"

Ana gave a choking sob, and Nikki's heart went out to her. She gentled her voice. "You said some of the staff left. Did they leave unexpectedly? Is there a chance someone is buried with the horses?"

"Maybe," Ana admitted. She dropped on the straw bales, her voice twisting with anguish. "But I can't say anything. Jorge has a sister in Texas. Durant threatened to kill her."

"He can't do anything if he's in prison."

"But the police might not even charge him. I can't risk it."

"Justin is a homicide detective. He can tell us the best approach."

"But it will take too long. It's too risky."

Nikki fought her frustration. Ana might never be persuaded to talk. True, legal channels would be slow and possibly ineffectual, especially considering Durant's control of the local police. But it went against her code to stand back and let him get away with murder.

"Are the horses buried on the south side?" she asked, remembering the headstones she'd spotted yesterday. There'd also been a monument, although there hadn't seemed to be any fresh dirt. "Are the graves marked with headstones?"

"Not anymore," Ana said dully. "Old Mr. Durant had monuments for his best studs. He honored some other horses with headstones. But that all stopped when he died and his son took over. Now the horses are just walked into the woods."

Ana raised her head, her eyes moist with unshed tears. "Some of the horses they took away were healthy. They just weren't fast enough to satisfy Durant. Chico would always be upset when he heard the gunshots... He seemed to know."

Nikki sank down beside Ana, absorbing this new information.

"Do you know the location in the woods?" she asked.

"No. They did it in the morning when we were working with the horses. And the property is huge. I've never been brave enough to follow any of the trails. But Gloria was."

"Did she tell you anything?"

"No, but I could see she was frightened. A week later, she disappeared. She might have gone back to Panama...but no one has heard from her."

Ana stopped talking, the pensive silence punctuated by Chico's rhythmic chewing. Moments later, she spoke again. "You said the arm was from a man, not a woman. That gives me hope."

It didn't leave Nikki very hopeful. Perhaps Gloria was safe; however, she feared there was an unfortunate soul buried somewhere on Durant's property. Maybe more than one. But at least Ana was talking.

"Did anybody else not show up for work? Unexpectedly?"

"Staff came and went all the time," Ana said. "In the winter, workers drifted down from the north. Most of them left in the spring."

"Because of the weather?"

"No, bigger tracks have higher purses and most trainers pay a bonus when their horses win. Durant only wants the prestige of winning. He's not like his father. He would never pay bonuses."

Or honor worker contracts, Nikki thought. Yet in spite of all the barriers, Ana had succeeded in guiding Chico to a successful string of races. And put Durant in the rare position of losing his horse to an employee.

"Can we talk more about this later?" Ana said. "I need to stay calm, for Chico's sake."

Nikki nodded, already weighing the possibility of obtaining a search warrant. But there wasn't enough evidence. Only a picture of an unidentified arm in an unidentified location, along with the whispers of employees who were too frightened to talk. The local police were in Durant's pocket so it would come down to Nikki's word against theirs, and a private investigator had little clout with the FBI. Maybe she and Gunner could sneak onto the property and find actual human bones.

The thought made her skin crawl. She wasn't eager to take Gunner back onto Durant's property with its gun-wielding guards. He had barely recuperated from his last bullet. It would be too risky to sneak in there alone. Justin would never help or condone that sort of action, knowing any police evidence obtained would be useless.

"Just one last question," she said. "I spotted a surveillance camera at the back of Durant's driveway. Are there any more near the woods where they take the horses?"

"Yes, that's one of the reasons Gloria was so spooked."

"So Durant must have known she was there. And she disappeared a week later?"

"*Dieu*! Can't you give it up. Going after Durant isn't healthy."

Nikki grinned. Tenacity was an essential quality for an investigator. But she didn't want to upset Ana and understood why the woman didn't want to handle Chico when she was distressed. Horses picked up on emotions even faster than dogs.

"I won't talk about Durant again today," she said, still smiling. "What can I do to help Chico win? Maybe take Gunner to the paddock and scare the favorite?"

Ana laughed, finally relaxing. But her gaze lifted to a spot behind Nikki and she instantly sobered. Nikki swung around.

Rick stood behind them, his forehead creased in a dark scowl. He didn't seem to realize she'd been joking about scaring competitors' horses. His arms were crossed, the tattoos stretched over his bulging muscles. The man didn't need a gun to look forbidding.

"You and your dog aren't going near the paddock," he snapped. "You're staying right here. So even if you attract Durant, there won't be any threat to innocents."

Including being a threat to his wife, Nikki thought. And the fact that he was still worried about Durant fanned her own concern.

"Is the jockeys' room secure?" she asked.

"Yes. But the race isn't run in the jock room. And I can't look after everyone."

He was a natural protector and clearly bothered by his limitations. The racetrack was a huge area and Chico and his rider would necessarily be exposed. If Eve were hurt in the post parade, it would be too late to replace the jockey and Chico would be scratched. Durant would win.

"Gunner and I can look after Ana," she said, using her most reasonable tone. "That will leave you free to concentrate on your wife."

Truthfully she wanted to run into Durant, to find him when he wasn't in a position of power. He might never answer to a court:

However, he'd tried to kill Gunner, had nearly raped her, and she had a score to settle. Her hands fisted in anticipation.

"You can't take that dog over by the grandstand," Rick said. "And you can't leave him unattended. So you're staying here. Where I won't have to worry about your motivations."

She widened her eyes, pretending she didn't know what he was talking about. But he wasn't fooled, nor was he moved by her frustrated huff.

When Rick turned to Ana, his voice softened. "If you and Jorge want any help in the paddock, I'll have some people on standby. Just let me know what you need. Good luck."

He strode down the shedrow, pausing to give last-minute instructions to his security guards who nodded and looked at him as if he were a walking god.

Ana watched Rick with a similar expression. "Mr. Talbot is a good man," she whispered, even though he was much too far away to hear.

Perceptive too, Nikki thought. And he wasn't that good of a man. He wouldn't have let Chico run if his wife hadn't committed to ride.

In actuality, she now realized Rick had a lawless streak, playing by the rules only when it suited him. And she could roll with that, if only she knew his rules. It was deflating how he'd taken over Chico's safety while sticking her far from the action. He seemed to view both her and Gunner as undisciplined. Indeed, she wanted to find Durant and cause him some pain, but most anyone would crave payback. Especially after last night.

She rubbed her hands over her arms, remembering her helplessness, how Durant had made her feel so worthless. And how dangerously close he'd come to killing Gunner.

"Don't be upset," Ana said. "You should be happy that track security is taking over. Besides, the starting gate will be in the chute so you'll still be able to see the beginning of the race. Chico will be in the one hole, next to the rail. He'll need a good break. Otherwise he'll be blocked in, and that's not how he likes to run."

Nikki pushed away the memory of Durant's sadistic laugh—the clinking of his ugly buckle—and focused on Ana. "How does Chico like to run?"

"Up with the frontrunners," Ana said. "There's usually both strategy and luck involved. If he's pinched back, he won't be able to make up the ground. His heart is willing but he doesn't have the closing kick of some of the younger horses.

"Even if he is up front, if the race goes too fast he won't have the energy to fight off the closers. Hopefully, Eve can control the pace. But she can only do that if Chico comes out of the gate like a bullet."

"Does Eve know your tactics? How she needs to ride to give Chico his best chance?"

"Yes, she's a pro," Ana said. "She's in the jockey room now watching videos of his past races. She also phoned Gary in the hospital and listened to all his tips. The plan is to hustle Chico out of the gate and grab a good position. This is the only race that starts in the chute so there's a long straight stretch to the first turn. And Chico is very calm so he's not wasting energy. He doesn't have a stable mate with him but Gunner is keeping him relaxed."

That part was certainly true. Chico was munching hay, looking as nonchalant as if he were home nibbling grass in the paddock. Gunner lay by his stall door, every bit as relaxed. Clumps of wet hay and saliva dotted his hair, and he rolled onto his side, seeming to think Chico might give him a belly rub.

Nikki pulled out her freshly charged phone and clicked a picture to send to Justin. He wouldn't see it until he was finished with his court prep but he'd be reassured that Gunner was behaving. Maybe Sonja was right and Gunner had been reacting to Nikki's emotions. He was certainly happier having a job.

The fun was almost over though. Soon, security would escort Ana and Chico to the paddock. Eve was safe in the jock room. The only way Durant could stop Chico now was with a bullet, and he didn't want the horse dead. He just wanted to make sure Chico lost.

An equipment malfunction might do that. Nikki's gaze shot to Jorge's saddle and the colorful foam pad draped over the drying rack. The crowded rack was twenty feet away and unattended. But then she remembered Eve would use her own race saddle. They were smaller and lighter than exercise saddles and kept in the jock room. So the only equipment here was Chico's bridle.

"Don't worry," Ana said, gesturing at a spot beside her where a white bridle gleamed. "Jorge already cleaned the bridle and I've double checked all the buckles and stitching. There's nothing left to do but wait."

Nikki sank back down beside Ana. "Is waiting for a race always this nerve-wracking?"

"Yes."

CHAPTER SIXTEEN

N ikki had spent much of her short career waiting. Surveillance was an integral part of investigative work and she'd learned how to calm her brain. But waiting for race eight was far different than sitting in a car, concealed behind a hat and sunglasses, watching an unknown subject.

She cared about Ana and Jorge. And every one of her senses buzzed.

Some of the tension was wondering if Durant would strike. She also was hobbled because she couldn't see the track. She could only hear and smell and imagine. Long periods of silence were punctuated by pounding hooves and the roar of the crowd, followed by bustling grooms as they led their horses back from their respective races.

The restless horse in the stall next to Chico had already returned after running in the second race. His disappointed groom reported he'd faded to last after leading most of the way.

By Nikki's calculation, it was now race seven. And with the passing of each race, her excitement grew. She wasn't the only one feeling the stress. Ana was chewing at her nails and Jorge kept polishing the same piece of leather.

"Shouldn't you start getting ready?" she asked.

"Ten more minutes," Ana said. "I want to stay away from Chico as long as possible. So he doesn't anticipate the race and waste energy worrying. Can you watch him for a minute while I go to the washroom?"

Nikki nodded, keeping her gaze on Chico as Ana hurried away. There was no worry about Chico wasting energy; he appeared to be in a Zen state. Both he and Gunner looked half asleep, the horse either not caring or unaware that his big race was inching closer.

His people knew though and Nikki couldn't stop bouncing on her toes. Now she understood Justin's passion for the sport. She'd accompanied him to the races, cheered enthusiastically for his horses, but had never experienced such a flurry of butterflies. Had always been more interested in riding a horse than watching them gallop in circles.

But after being immersed in Chico's life, she was now totally captivated. And she ached to watch the race with Ana. To stand beside her and Jorge and help cheer Chico on to a win. It seemed as if they were marching into battle without her. And what if Durant made a move?

"I thought a big city PI like you wouldn't get nervous before a little race." Rick's amused voice sounded behind her. "You need to control your nerves. It can pass on to your dog. And the horse."

The man moved way too silently. And he still considered her and Gunner a liability. His opinion of her shouldn't sting. But it did.

"As you can see," she said, jabbing a thumb at the dozing animals, "they're totally relaxed. As am I."

Rick looked at the marks her restless feet had made and arched a sardonic eyebrow. "I know you're not happy about being stuck back here. But you can still watch the start. The guard will accompany you. Just cut between the two barns, and the horse path will take you right to the chute."

"But there's no way to see the finish from there," she said, no longer trying to hide her excitement. "And Ana will be alone."

"My men will protect her. And your phone is charged now. The full race card is live streamed."

"How about if I walk over to the side of the grandstand? Just for Chico's race?"

"And if you run into Durant? Can you promise not to approach him? That you'll back off and call me?"

She thought a little too long before answering.

His mouth tightened. "I can't let this track turn into a battlefield, Nikki."

"But Durant is scum. And possibly a murderer. He systemically rapes his workers and encourages his brutes to do the same. Then threatens them with deportation if they complain. I'm not going to let him get away with it."

"That's exactly the reckless behavior that got you in trouble last night. Knowing when to fight is just as important as the courage to take action. And that wasn't the right time to go after him."

"But Durant tried to poison my dog. Of course, I went after him!"

Gunner scrambled to his feet, alarmed by her rising voice. His abrupt movement startled Chico who flung his head, nostrils flaring. His knee struck the wooden door, the loud rap sounding along the aisle and frightening the horse in the adjacent stall.

"Now you and your dog are getting the horses all excited." Rick made a disapproving sound deep in this throat. "That's one of the reasons we have rules about creds and why only genuine service dogs are allowed. Like I said, this isn't the place to settle scores. And there's no need for you to worry about Ana. If Durant or any of his men show up, I'll have them detained until the races are over."

"On what grounds?"

"I'll find something." Rick grinned, his smile rather wicked. "After all, he's the registered owner of a horse with an unlicensed groom. One who's a little too keen to right all the wrongs in the world. All by herself, any way she can."

Nikki scowled, knowing further protest was useless. Rick had made up his mind about her and Gunner. He didn't want their help. She had no qualms about his ability. He was smart, savvy, and had armed men at his disposal, along with instant communication.

And his insight about her personal vendetta was undeniable. She wanted to see Durant, wanted to make him pay. For raping Ana, for crippling helpless horses, and for trying to kill Gunner. The man might never set foot in a court house. But she didn't want him to get away scot free.

Rick shifted sideways, speaking into his mouthpiece. Judging by his terse commands, it sounded like she'd have a guard by her side all afternoon. Which meant Gunner would have to remain tied to the stall door. He'd hate that, especially if Chico were gone.

It would also be impossible to hear the call of the race. At this distance, the announcements were muffled. She certainly wasn't going to walk over to the chute and leave Gunner tied to the stall, exposed to Durant, unable to protect himself. He'd be too vulnerable. She'd heard enough horror stories of tethered K9s being shot or strangled to death by their own leashes.

"Stay alert," Rick said, turning off his mic. "Rats like Durant can turn even more vindictive when things don't go their way."

"We agree on that," she muttered, her frustration leaking out.

"Take this." He pressed a leash into her hand. "Use it when you walk over to the chute."

She fingered the thick leather. So it seemed she was allowed to take Gunner to the chute even though he'd avoided giving specific permission. That was a nice concession although it was odd she couldn't use her own leash.

This one seemed designed for a rhino, with an enormous brass snap that had probably been borrowed from a stud shank. Her eyes narrowed on the heavy snap, outwardly strong but attached by a fragile string...and something that would break away with the slightest amount of pressure.

A fake leash. And utterly perfect for enabling Gunner to protect himself.

"Wow." She grinned up at Rick, feeling much better. "You're not so strict after all."

"Sure I am. But only when it comes to stubborn investigators. Your dog is actually good at following orders."

Her smile deepened. Rick didn't give away praise lightly. They both knew stubborn was a necessary quality for investigators. And if he hadn't noticed that Gunner was hostile with men, she wasn't going to mention it. Now at least she could watch the start of Chico's race, with her dog safe beside her.

"Thank you," she said. "I'm really excited about the race, way more than I expected to be."

"Not surprising. You worked hard to keep that horse safe. Fake creds and all."

Despite his deadpan expression, his eyes twinkled, proving he really had softened. And he had praised her dog. If he was no longer worried about Gunner biting someone, maybe he'd reconsider and let her mingle with the spectators.

"Instead of watching from the chute," she asked, "could Gunner and I walk over to the grandstand? Where we can see the finish? Would that be okay?"

"No," he said.

CHAPTER SEVENTEEN

Twenty-nine...thirty. Nikki finished another series of pushups, determined to keep busy and not worry about Ana and Chico. Right now, they were probably in the paddock where horses gathered for saddling and to meet with their jockeys. Then the Thoroughbreds would parade in front of the grandstand so spectators could see the runners and make a bet or two.

She rolled onto her back, reminding herself that Chico was well-protected. After coming this far though, it was hard to relinquish control. Unfortunately Rick was adamant she stay away from the public area. He'd even left a guard to make sure she obeyed.

Not that she needed one. She'd accepted it wouldn't be possible to cheer Chico on in person. Or even back him with a bet. Even if she could make it to a betting window, her money and credit cards were back at the cabin.

Gunner gave her shoulder an impatient nudge. He hadn't been pleased when Ana had led Chico away, the horse all dressed up in his gleaming white bridle and carefully taped legs. Chico had looked back at Gunner, as if questioning why his buddy wasn't coming. Then he'd swung his head around and continued his stately walk, seemingly aware he had to run the race on his own.

Nikki sat up and wrapped her arm around Gunner's neck. "We'll walk over to the chute soon. At least we can watch the start. And we have the internet."

She checked her phone's video feed. The picture was tiny though and didn't show the paddock, only the faces of two race analysts discussing the odds of each horse. Bettors weren't giving Chico much love. At forty to one, he was the longest shot on the board.

But Ana didn't put much stock in the odds. And obviously Durant thought Chico had a puncher's chance since the man had gone to such drastic lengths to stop him from running.

Nikki stared at the numbers, running some quick calculations. It was unfortunate Ana had no money to risk because, if by some miracle Chico did win, the payout would be huge. Horse transport to Chile wasn't cheap. And it seemed like a glaring oversight, along with a total lack of faith, not to back the horse.

Though she couldn't make it to the pari-mutuel window, there was always an online option. But lacking any ID or credit cards, she'd need help to set up a betting account. Justin hadn't replied to her most recent text but Sonja had.

She quickly pressed Sonja's number and updated her on the situation.

"So you want my help to bet on a possible winner," Sonja teased. "I'm surprised you don't want my psychic opinion first."

"I'd ask you to talk to the horse," Nikki said. "But he isn't here."

"You've come a long way, my friend."

Nikki didn't argue. She didn't understand her friend's gift but Sonja had been right too many times to ignore. "Can you talk to him from a distance?" Nikki asked. "Find out if he's going to win?"

"You know animals aren't my thing."

"But you did it with Sparky."

"That was different. You had the phone beside him and I only picked up the beagle's vibes. You're asking me to reach a horse. And how would he know if he's going to win? The most I could find out is if he's feeling good."

"We know he's feeling good," Nikki said. "I just don't want to lose my money."

"A gambler's risk. And if I could see this type of outcome, I'd be retired and living in Barbados. But I'm setting up the betting account now.

"Done," she said, after a moment. "I used my credit card to deposit the money. What's his name and I'll lay your bet."

"Chico's Kid, race eight. He's the number one horse."

"Okay." Sonja's voice trailed off, her silence rather foreboding.

"What is it?" Nikki paced a circle on the grass. Sonja's silences often meant she was seeing something. Maybe that Durant was going to sabotage Chico's race?

"Just a sec," Sonja said.

Nikki pressed her lips together, waiting for what seemed an eternity.

"Your horse is feeling good," Sonja finally said. "But he's looking at a younger horse. Thinks that horse is stronger and faster, possibly a bit green. Can you bet on them both?"

"Sure," Nikki said. The payoff would be even higher for Ana if they included another horse. "We can bet an exacta. What's the other horse's number?"

"Beats me," Sonja said. "Chico doesn't know numbers."

Of course he doesn't, Nikki thought, rubbing the back of her neck. But it was impossible to narrow it down since all the horses in the race were younger than Chico. There was one three-year-old in the field. The rest were four and five, with Chico the oldest at age seven. He probably didn't know colors either, at least not as the program listed them.

Nikki sighed. "It's too hard to guess who he's talking about. Better just bet on Chico to come second then. Is that the only horse he's afraid of?"

"He's not afraid of him," Sonja said. "He just thinks the horse is fast. And Chico doesn't like him. The horse is right behind him, showing off for the crowd and threatening to bite his bum. Chico is going to kick his head off if he gets any closer."

They must be in the post parade, Nikki thought, checking the entries again, brightening when she saw that the number two horse was a three-year-old. That had to be the horse behind Chico.

"This is fun," Sonja went on. "Chico is talking trash. And the number two horse is intimidated and has backed off."

Perfect. If the young horse felt subordinate to Chico, he might back off in the race too. Even a moment's hesitation could make a difference.

"Okay," Nikki said. "So bet the exactor with Chico to win. And the number two horse to come second."

She kept an anxious eye on the screen as Sonja struggled to find the right buttons to press. Eighteen minutes to post.

"Done," Sonja finally said. "The bet was accepted. And because it's a new account, we have a complimentary two hundred dollar credit."

"That's yours to bet," Nikki said. "Put it wherever you want. Maybe you'll hit the jackpot and be able to finish your veranda."

"Cool. I've never bet on horses before. I have to figure out who Chico thinks will come third. That would pay big. Or maybe I could pick the first four finishers. Do they have to come in the exact order?"

"Yes, unless you wheel them all, and that costs a lot more."

The security guard gestured from the end of the shedrow, signaling that it was time to walk toward the chute.

"Don't wait too long," Nikki said, scooping up the end of Gunner's leash and heading toward the waiting guard. "The race is starting soon."

"Gotta go," Sonja said. "Have to get back into Chico's head. Figure out the superfecta before betting is blocked. He has strong opinions about all the horses. I feel a big payday coming!"

She cut the connection so fast it left Nikki laughing. She and Justin had never been able to persuade Sonja to join them at the track. Yet now the terms Sonja was throwing out made her sound as passionate as any hardcore race fan.

CHAPTER EIGHTEEN

Nikki leaned over the rail, peering to her right, straining to see the parading horses. From this distance, the grandstand looked tiny and the jockeys were only splashes of color on the horses' backs.

But as the horses began their warm-up, they moved closer. She was too far away to see the numbers on the saddlecloths, but Chico's white bridle and leg wraps were distinctive, along with Eve's yellow and white silks.

She blew out a quiet breath of relief. Chico had made it out of the paddock, past the crowd, and out of Durant's reach. Soon they'd turn and head toward the starting gate that the tractor had positioned in the chute, only thirty feet from where she and the guard stood.

This was actually a great spot to watch the beginning of the race; the starting gate was so close she could see the padding on its steel sides. Chico was number one so he'd break from the stall closest to the inside rail. And the young horse Sonja had pegged as the fastest would be beside him in the two hole.

She stretched further over the rail, studying the crowd in front of the grandstand. Somewhere in that noisy throng, Ana and Jorge were watching. No doubt they were still nervous about the upcoming race but at least Chico was safe from Durant. A triumph in itself.

"You need to step back now," the security guard said. "Rick wants you and your dog well off the rail."

She obligingly moved back several feet, guiding Gunner behind her. The last thing she'd ever want to do was scare a horse. And while she relished this moment and how Chico had successfully made it to the gate, a part of her still worried about Durant. She'd expected that such a vindictive man would have made another attempt to stop Chico.

"Did anything unusual happen?" she asked. "In the saddling area?"

"I wasn't there," the guard said, folding his muscled arms over his chest. "I was with you and your dog."

And he wasn't happy about his job, she realized. Like her, he preferred to be closer to the action. He actually looked like he could be a player in an action movie, not babysitting her and Gunner.

Her eyes narrowed. This wasn't the paunchy guard who had delivered the coffee. Or the short guy who'd been posted at the shedrow in the afternoon. In fact, she couldn't remember seeing this man.

The original guard had signaled that the race was starting soon. Had urged her to hurry. But she'd been talking to Sonja at the time and hadn't noticed why the men had switched. She'd assumed this guard was part of the track's regular security team. The khaki uniform matched. However, the muscular body inside didn't. In fact, the uniform looked a size too small, as if it had been grabbed in a hurry.

She edged toward the guard's holster, checking his reaction. He automatically shifted, protecting his gun. The other guards hadn't been nearly as vigilant. They also had referred to Rick as "Boss." None of them ever called Rick by name, not within her hearing.

She swallowed. They were so close to the gate. And the last chance to hurt a jockey, to stop a horse from running. It seemed Durant hadn't given up after all.

"Have you worked at the track long?" she asked, stroking Gunner's head, pretending the answer wasn't at all important.

"I don't work here," the guard said. "Just doing a favor."

Her hand stilled behind Gunner's ear but the guard wasn't watching her reaction. He was eyeing the gate crew. And his frown showed he wasn't happy with what he saw.

He tilted his head, speaking into a clip-on microphone. "One extra crew member here, a female."

She listened, straining to make out the voice on the other end. Praying it wasn't Durant. Her heart steadied when she heard a familiar voice—Rick's not Durant. Heard Rick confirm that the extra person was the track vet. So this new guard was legit. She'd let her suspicious nature jump into overdrive.

The guard turned away, keeping the rest of his call private. When he returned to her side, he gave her a quizzical look. "Rick wants you to know," he said, "that your friends are fine. He's holding three men in the office so says to stop worrying and enjoy the race."

"Three men? Not four?"

"He said three." The guard dismissed her, his alert gaze swinging to the approaching horses. And their jockeys.

"So you're here to protect Eve," Nikki said.

"That's right. Rick called some friends, asked us to help out. This place is tighter than a drum. He even handpicked the assistant starters."

The idea that Durant might try to bribe one of the assistant starters hadn't even occurred to her. They had the challenging job of going in the stall with each horse, keeping them calm and helping them come out of the gate fairly. She had to admit that Rick was thorough. No wonder he hadn't wanted her help.

She folded her arms, watching the gate crew as they gathered around the rear of the starting gate, awaiting the horses. This was a restricted area so it was easier to monitor than the grandstand and paddock. All the people here seemed legit. Even the vet, the small woman who had initially raised the guard's concern, moved with intrinsic authority.

There was no one in sight who looked out of place. And the entire area, including a stand of trees at the end of the chute, was encased by a formidable fence. However, the trees also offered a good place to hide and she remembered how easily Durant handled razor wire.

"Were the trees checked for a shooter?" she asked.

The guard gave a dismissive grunt. "The ambulance blocks the sight line and the treed area is too low for a shot."

She glanced at the access road by the chute, noting how the ambulance and service vehicles had been strategically parked. It really seemed nothing could stop Chico now. Except bad luck.

And luck was often a factor, especially at the start. Sometimes horses stumbled because the ground gave way beneath the force of their propulsion. It was hard for a jockey to stay on when their horse's nose was scraping the ground. Chico needed a good start. But he was calm and experienced; supposedly he broke well.

Besides, it was impossible for Durant to control what happened in the starting gate.

Her eyes narrowed on the metal gate, positioned next to a red and white pole on the rail. Colorful numbers marked the top of each stall—numbers that had been pre-drawn. Ana had known for days that Chico had drawn the one hole.

She swung around to the guard. "Were you watching this spot earlier? Before we walked over?"

"No, I was sent directly to the shedrow. To accompany you."

She wheeled, catching the attention of an assistant starter who sported a handlebar moustache beneath his helmet. "Were you around the chute," she called, "before the tractor brought the gate?"

"No, we came after the gate was positioned."

"Does the gate always go in the same spot?"

"For a mile and a quarter race. They have to measure exact times so the poles are necessary to calculate distances."

"Does that mean you know where a horse would stand? In the gate?"

"It would be a rough guess," he said. "Except for the one hole since the gate is next to the rail."

He turned his attention to the approaching horses, blowing off any more of her questions.

"We need to call Rick," she said to the guard. "I think the gate should be checked. No one's been watching it."

"Unwarranted," the guard said. "The gate looks fine. It's right next to the pole."

"Yes, but what if someone tampered with it?"

"I'm not bothering Rick again," the guard said. "He has enough to worry about with his wife riding the target horse."

"Yes. And she's going in that gate. In the one hole. On your watch..." Nikki let her voice trail off because the guard was already reaching for his radio.

Three minutes later, Rick stepped out from his Jeep and hurried toward them.

"Circle the horses away from the gate," he said, speaking into his handset. "Wait for my all clear."

He clipped his radio back on his belt and stepped over the rail. "Keep an eye on Eve, Mike," he said. Then he looked at Nikki. "Come with me."

Obviously he wasn't brushing off her concern that Durant might have tampered with the gate, and the guard called Mike slanted his head in acknowledgement. She nodded back, grateful he'd backed her up. Then she and Gunner slipped beneath the rail and followed Rick.

"Ana said this was the only race starting in the chute today," she said, walking fast so as to keep up with Rick's long strides.

"That's right," he said, clearly not up for conversation.

Gunner trotted beside her. But he moved reluctantly and kept looking over his shoulder at the circling horses, aware Chico was close by.

"Come on," she said, disappointed by his lack of enthusiasm. Granted, he wasn't trained as a track-sniffing dog. She wasn't even sure how a gate could be booby trapped. Maybe mess with the opening mechanism? The start was critical for Chico, especially coming out of the one hole. If his door was slow to open, it would wreck his chances.

"What makes the stall doors open?" she asked. "Is it possible to make one door open slower?"

"That would take time and skill."

"But it could be done. It's magnetized, right?"

"Yes," Rick said, shooting her a sideways look. "But the doors have been opening perfectly all day. Seven fair starts. And the ground crew has been with the gate between races. No one had the chance to sabotage."

Then why had Rick driven over here, she thought. And paused the race. The horses wouldn't appreciate the delay. Nor would the trainers and fans. Then she remembered how carefully Ana had examined the floor in Chico's stall, worried he might step on something sharp.

"But no one was watching the chute," she said slowly. "So it must be the ground you came to check."

"And you must be an investigator," Rick said, and there was a hint of respect in his voice. "I just want to take a quick look. I should have thought of it myself."

He strode past the gate crew and into the first stall. The slot was narrow, barely wide enough for a horse to fit, and she marveled once again that horses could be trained to walk into such a contraption.

"We're both probably being overly suspicious," Rick said, kicking at the dirt with his boot. "Durant didn't even show up today, only his men. But it won't take long to check."

He dropped to his knees, his mutters changing to a curse.

"What is it?" She edged forward, trying to see past his wide shoulders.

"Glass," he said. "A lot of it."

He rose, gesturing at the concerned men. "Get the rakes. Check every slot. This section was harrowed this morning so the broken glass is recent." He brushed past Nikki, speaking into his microphone again.

Gunner whined, affected by the sudden tension. She guided him further behind the starting gate, away from the confusing smells of horses, humans and footprints. Closer to the cluster of trees near the end of the chute.

"What do you see?" she asked, using her singsong voice, trying to focus his attention on the trees, aware his leash was attached with a flimsy string. It wouldn't be very professional if he broke away and ran toward the horses, thinking he was supposed to find Chico. Spectators might enjoy the sight of a loose dog joining his horse buddy but Rick wouldn't be amused.

However, Gunner shoved his muzzle into the ground, sniffing at human prints. He lifted his head and growled, staring in the opposite direction of Chico. Toward the trees.

She felt Rick's scrutiny. "Let him loose," he called.

"You're sure?"

"Yes. That fucking psycho is messing with my track."

Nikki flicked the leash, snapping the string. "Find!"

And Gunner was free. He trotted half a loop, nose to the ground. Seconds later he turned and shot toward the woods.

She sprinted after him, not certain if anyone was still hiding in those trees, but driven by the need to stay close to her dog. Judging by Gunner's enthusiasm, it was more than some kids looking for free admission. Maybe Durant's men had been set up as a decoy, leaving Durant free to commit his carnage.

She entered the trees, her wary gaze darting left to right. She'd been lured into an ambush before and she certainly wasn't going to climb any fence and let herself be separated from Gunner.

He was still ahead of her but his excited barks sounded close. And then his barks turned to aggressive growls. It must be someone from last night for him to make that kind of noise.

She burst around a yellow-leafed ash tree and skidded to a stop, absorbing the scene.

The Armani jacket was familiar. So was the diamond-studded belt buckle, the one that made such a chilling sound in the dark. But today Durant was the person flattened in the dirt. He lay perfectly still, spread-eagled, as if he'd been admiring the view of the sky—except that Gunner's big jaws were wrapped around his crotch.

"Call off your dog," he snapped. "Or I'll kick his damn head off."

Even in a vulnerable position the man felt entitled, issuing threats and expecting instant compliance. And that left her even more eager to extract a pound of flesh. "Start kicking," she said.

She scanned the trees, reassuring herself that he was alone. Then stepped closer. "Go ahead and kick," she repeated. "He won't need much of an excuse. Clearly he remembers what happened last night."

"Nothing happened. And if he bites me, you're in bigger trouble than you already are."

"Seems you're the one in trouble." She crouched down, studying his face. Trying to see past his arrogance, to find some regret for the terror he'd inflicted. There was no guessing how many of his staff he'd abused. Ana wouldn't talk numbers; she didn't want to speak of it at all. But Durant's expression was empty of anything but outrage.

"Call your dog off," he demanded. "Or my lawyers will have him put down. I might do it anyway, just to teach you a lesson about helping that spic."

She stiffened. Gunner must have sensed her anger because his jaws tightened.

"Okay, okay," Durant's voice had a satisfying squeak. "Let me up. Whatever she's paying, I'll triple it."

"Her name is Ana."

"What are you? A bleeding heart like my father?" His snicker was quick and derisive. "Or did *Ana* promise you part of the horse? She'll never get him. And I can pay you more."

"Not everything is about money."

"Come on. Name your price. And maybe I'll let Ana go back to Mexico or wherever she's from. But the horse stays."

"Not if he wins today," Nikki said, studying Durant's reaction. "Legally she would own him."

"That horse is too old to win again. He should have been sent to stud last year. My father was a fool to saddle me with those agreements."

Nikki had never seen Ana's contract but it was reassuring that Durant wasn't questioning the terms. Only his father's generosity.

"Besides," Durant went on, "those people wouldn't know what to do with a stud like that. I only keep the women around for shoveling shit...and maybe a couple other things.

"Now turn and walk away," he said, misreading her silence. "Or my lawsuit will make your head swim. And I won't stop with your dog. In fact, I'll put you in a place where you won't do any more jogging."

"Are you talking about your secret burial grounds?" Nikki spoke through gritted teeth. "Is that the source of the bone I found?"

"Fuck off."

"The more I hear, the more I think that's a good idea." She straightened and stepped back. Gunner's jaws had a bite force of over five hundred pounds. Durant would be doing a lot of thrashing. She didn't want to get in the way.

"Hey, what are you doing?"

"Walking away, just like you asked. Soon women everywhere will be safer."

"Wait!" Durant's arrogance finally seemed to have been pierced. "Call off your dog. Maybe then I'll forget your interference."

"And forget how you raped Ana? Your other employees? How you tried to rape me!" Heat flushed through her body. "I can't forget that."

"But you can't let your dog eat me. Call him off!"

Gunner watched, waiting for her signal while Durant spit out a slew of physical and legal threats. He had money and power, and would be a dangerous foe. But at least Ana and the missing Gloria would have some justice.

Footsteps sounded behind her. Gunner wasn't alarmed so Nikki knew it must be Rick.

"You can't stop me," she said, checking over her shoulder.

"Not planning to," Rick said.

"He deserves this."

"Yes, but first I need to talk to him." Rick moved past her, calmly crouching down and checking Durant's pockets, his legs, and the back of that ostentatious belt.

"Did you hide glass anywhere else on the track?" he asked, ignoring Gunner, as if accustomed to interrogating men who had jaws clamped around their genitals.

"No," Durant snapped. "Just the first stall. What took security so long to show up? That woman's crazy. Now get the damn dog off me."

"Do you have anyone set up to take pot shots at the horse?" Rick asked. "Or the jockey?"

"No, I thought the glass would be enough. Now get rid of that vicious animal before he bites. You have a gun." He shot Nikki a malicious smile. "Fifty thousand dollars if you shoot him now. In front of her."

"What you don't understand is that my wife is riding Chico," Rick said. "So, I'm going to ask one more time, and I need an honest answer. Are you absolutely sure the race is safe to run?"

"Yes, I swear. Now shoot that dog. His teeth are squeezing my balls."

"I'm not finished with my questions," Rick said, his voice gentle. "I'd like to hear more about your methods, how you abused employees so they'd run off."

"Aren't you a fucking security guard? You're not allowed to ask questions while I'm being threatened. Do your job. Shoot that dog."

Rick eyed Gunner thoughtfully as if just noticing the jaw hold. Clearly he'd insist that she call her dog off. But he didn't speak. His only movement was a muscle ticking in his jaw, and she realized that what she'd mistaken for gentleness was actually controlled fury.

And seeing his emotion, knowing that he shared her anger, made her feel much calmer. Her entire body seemed to cool.

"Sometimes it's impossible to call off a dog," Rick said, looking back at Durant. "My dogs don't always listen either. And that's totally understandable...under the circumstances."

Durant blanched.

"I actually saw you and your men last night," Rick went on, his voice menacing in its softness. "Noted it in my log book. It's my opinion a dog could be forgiven for a bite. Or two."

"What the hell," Durant sputtered. "Who *are* you people?"

Rick ignored Durant and looked at Nikki. "You can let Gunner give you some personal satisfaction," he said. "Or walk away and let me handle this. But decide quickly. Because my men are going to be here soon. And some things are best done without witnesses." He gave Durant a humorless smile. "As I'm sure this scumbag will attest."

Durant's eyes widened. "Help! Someone help me! They're both crazy—"

His shouts trickled to a whimper. Gunner was reacting to Durant's hollers and began squeezing his jaws, as if playing with a tennis ball. Nikki remained silent. She didn't want to call him off. Likely Durant's lawyers would keep him out of court, and this might be the only chance to extract some vengeance.

"So," Rick said, his voice turning urgent. "Do you and Gunner want to leave? Will you trust me to handle this? To try to make it right?"

It was both surprising and empowering that he was giving her the choice, as if he understood how it felt to be a victim. She swallowed, trying to steady her emotions, to think rationally. Obviously it would be safer for Gunner if they left but the opportunity to punish Durant was heady.

Would Rick let Durant walk away with a slap on the wrist? She remembered how protective he was: of Eve, of his people, of the track community. And it didn't take long to come up with her answer.

"Guess it wouldn't be healthy for Gunner to bite something so rotten," she said.

"Probably not."

"And you are head of track security. So we'll leave and let you handle it."

Rick stared at her for a moment then gave an approving nod and reached for his radio.

"The race is safe to proceed," he said, speaking into the mouthpiece. "But send a car to deliver a VIP guest to the clubhouse. She'll be accompanied by her service dog."

CHAPTER NINETEEN

———◦———

"This is an all-access pass," the female official said, presenting Nikki with two badges attached to a colorful lanyard. Her gaze flickered to the rearview mirror, eyeing Gunner who filled the rear seat of the Jeep. "The second badge goes on your dog's leash. You can go anywhere, on both the front and backside."

"Great." Nikki looped the badge around her neck then attached the second one to Gunner's leash. "Does that mean we can stand by the rail? With the other spectators?"

"Of course. You can also enjoy complimentary food and drinks at any of the bars. Not sure about the restaurant though." The woman studied Gunner with a mixture of wariness and confusion. "I've never seen Boss give out these before, and that is one imposing shepherd. Anyway if you hurry, you should be able to catch the stakes race. They're starting to load the horses in the gate."

"Thanks." Nikki whipped open the door of the Jeep hurried toward the surging crowd.

People clustered everywhere. Many were at ground level while others were packed in the grandstand or had premium seats high in the clubhouse behind a wall of glass. The spectators to her right pressed around the rail. Some gripped programs, others balanced beer and hotdogs, their attention riveted on a giant infield screen that showed horses being led into the starting gate.

Nikki veered to the right, guessing that Ana would be watching close to the finish line. A tall usher stepped forward, blocking her way, his horrified scowl on Gunner. The frown disappeared when he spotted the badge around Gunner's leash.

"May I help you find your box?" he asked politely. "There's an elevator to the clubhouse just inside the doors. I can escort you."

"No thanks. I'm joining friends by the rail." She gave him a quick smile and hurried past, afraid she'd miss the race.

Spectators were clustered five-thick but they moved sideways when they saw Gunner, opening up a narrow passageway. Still, there were a lot of people, and Ana and Jorge were too short to spot. She paused, accepting she'd never find them in time; the infield screen showed there were only two horses left to load.

But Gunner forged ahead and as more people edged away, she glimpsed Ana and Jorge, only fifteen feet away. They had a prime spot by the finish line. Both of them were leaning over the rail, their attention fixed on the starting gate.

She squeezed in beside Ana. "What a great view."

"What are you doing here? How did you sneak Gunner in?" Ana's eyes widened but she was too intent on the race to wait for an explanation. "The race was delayed for some reason," she said, her head swiveling back toward the chute. "But Chico stayed calm. He's in the gate now, standing quietly. I can see all four of his feet."

Ana was vibrating with so much excitement that her words ran together. Jorge was in a similar state. He gave Gunner's head a quick pat, all the while rocking back and forth on his toes.

"I can't watch." Ana ducked her head, her hands white-knuckled over the rail. *"Por favor Dios,* let him have a good break. But that horse in the three hole is super quick."

Their nervousness was contagious and Nikki pulled in a deep breath. They didn't have to worry about Durant any longer but Chico still had to win. The odds board showed that the speedy three horse was a co-favorite. Chico had to come out fast or he'd be squeezed out.

"The horses are in the gate," the announcer said.

Ana made a choking sound.

"They're off!" the announcer called.

The crowd roared. Nikki gripped Gunner's leash and leaned over the rail, trying to see down the long expanse of dirt. It looked like a fair start with all the horses in a straight line across the track. Then a bay horse with red blinkers took over but just to his inside, snug against the rail, was Chico.

"Good break," Ana said, jumping up and down. "He's keeping the rail."

The horses galloped toward them, Chico's white bridle easily recognizable. He looked small next to the other horses, but he seemed to be running comfortably. The red-blinkered horse next to him was pulling at his bridle and running with flattened ears, as if daring him to pass. Chico wasn't intimidated. He kept his prime spot on the rail, sticking like a burr to the other horse's shoulder.

They swept past them in a cluster of pounding hooves, streaming tails and jockeys' shouts, the horse with the red blinkers leading by a neck. Gunner shoved against Nikki's thigh, ears pricked, seeming to understand that Chico was in that herd of racing horses.

She pulled her eyes off the race for a quick second, long enough to give him a reassuring pat. People all around them hollered with excitement and a big man leaned over her shoulder, urging a horse in the back to dig in. But Gunner remained unfazed, as if realizing that the cheering spectators posed no threat.

She turned her attention back to the race. The horses entered the clubhouse turn, with Chico saving ground on the rail, content to let the horse in the red blinkers lead the way. Chico was galloping smoothly, listening to his jockey, while the horse in front still pulled at his bridle, insisting on running faster. That horse won't be around at the finish, Nikki thought. The race was too long to waste energy fighting a rider.

"Keep the rail," Ana was calling. "Make him work for it."

Nikki switched her gaze to the infield screen, finding it easier to watch the action there than to stare at the muddle of horses on the backside. A black horse had powered his way to the front, joining the red-blinkered horse on the lead while Eve was keeping Chico on the rail, making the other two run wide.

Nikki gripped the rail, her knuckles now as white at Ana's. It was good Chico was saving ground. For a mile and a quarter race, he'd have to conserve energy. And he was still running easily, not boxed in or fighting his rider.

Her gaze swung back and forth from the screen to the live action on the far side of the track, too excited to settle on one view.

Ana abruptly jammed her arm in the air. "Look! The other two are giving up. They're fading."

Indeed, the other two horses were falling back, despite their jockeys' urging. Now Chico was in the lead and the horse with the red blinkers dropped to his hip. The black horse that had shot up, but ran wide the entire time, had backed off to fifth.

The horses rounded the final turn and headed down the home stretch with Chico leading the way. Nikki jumped up and down beside Ana, calling encouragement, even though she'd intended to remain calm, for Gunner's sake. But everyone around her was cheering on their favorite horse and Gunner didn't seem bothered. In fact, he was one of the few spectators dignified enough to remain silent.

"Watch out for the gray!" Ana's voice rose in urgency. "He's coming!"

Nikki wasn't sure if Ana was talking to Eve or Chico, and obviously they couldn't hear her. There were two gray horses in the field including the six horse who was the other co-favorite. But that horse was still at the rear, stuck behind a wall of fading runners.

It was the second gray horse moving up on the outside. His jockey wore bright yellow colors with number two on his saddle pad. And he appeared to be flying past the other horses with energy to spare.

"Please, help Chico finish. *Por favor.*" Ana covered her eyes and was speaking Spanish now. She reached out, desperately gripping Nikki's arm, but it wasn't enough to anchor Nikki. She and Jorge both rocked in anguish, pleading for Chico to hang on.

However, the late-running gray horse was closing like a freight train. And Chico had run so fast, for so long, and the finish line was still a hundred feet away.

And though he was clearly straining with every bit of his huge heart, and Eve was riding with steely determination, the gray horse pushed up to Chico's nose. For an instant he was beside him. Then the grey surged past. And Nikki felt like crying because the finish line was so close and she'd never seen such a brave little horse. The odds of Chico winning had always been high but it hurt that Durant was going to win after all.

A lump clogged her throat, and she and Ana fell silent. For a respectful moment even the loud man behind her quieted as they all watched the courageous little brown horse continue to run his heart out. Refusing to quit.

But running second.

And then Gunner rose on his hind legs, shoved his head over the rail and barked, an odd sound she'd never heard before. Almost like encouragement. And Chico flattened his ears, strained forward and stuck his nose back in front of that gray horse as if he'd known all along where the finish line was and had just been saving up for a last Herculean effort.

"He did it!" Ana shouted. "We won. *Gracias! Gracias!*"

She started jumping and crying and laughing all at the same time while Jorge grinned in disbelief. And smiling strangers patted them on their backs and shook their hands, and the man behind Nikki gave her an enthusiastic fist bump even though the horse he'd been cheering for had finished last.

Ana thrust her hands in the air and bounced toward the winner's circle, waving at them to follow.

But Nikki wasn't ready to join the official celebration. Not quite yet. Blinking back her own tears, she dropped to her knees. And hugged her wonderful dog.

EPILOGUE

Nikki leaned back on the cushioned chair, cupping her coffee and relishing the morning sun. The view from Sonja's porch had always been enjoyable but the new wraparound veranda offered stunning views of both the eastern and western sky. Considering her current company, there was no other place she'd rather be. It wasn't often that all her favorite animals and people were gathered in one spot.

"He's a special guy," Sonja said, gesturing at the trio relaxed on the grass below. Gunner lay on his back, paws in the air, carefree as a puppy while Justin scratched his belly. They were watched by a scruffy gray pony who kept nudging Justin's arm, impatient for his turn.

Nikki blew out a contented sigh. Sonja could have been talking about the man, the dog or the pony. Didn't matter. They were all special and it was a pleasure to have everyone together. This interlude wouldn't last long. Justin's phone had been ringing non-stop and it appeared he'd have to return to the city and take over a stalled murder case.

"You and Justin should stay more often," Sonja said. "It's better than renting a cabin in the woods. And there are no creepy bones to wreck a vacation."

Nikki just smiled. She didn't regret the time spent with Ana and Chico. Not one bit. Helping vulnerable people was one of the reasons she'd become an investigator. And though it hadn't been a paying job, she'd left feeling richly rewarded. About the case. About Gunner. About herself.

"It all worked out," she said. "Ana finally owns Chico. And Gunner had the chance to prove he was fit to return to work. Crowds don't bother him. Men either. He listened to every command. You wouldn't believe how good he was."

"Sure I do. I didn't doubt him for a minute."

"You were right," Nikki admitted, glancing sideways at her friend. "About his aggressiveness. He was picking up on my emotions. Reacting to them. I think Rick Talbot knew that as well."

"Is Rick the security guy?"

Nikki nodded. But Rick was much more than that. She'd learned that he'd been an undercover cop then later worked for an elite investigative company. That explained his contacts, his capabilities and his surprising openness to frontier justice. When he'd promised to "handle" Durant, he'd really meant it.

"You were in on it, weren't you?" Sonja said. "How those other bones were discovered on Durant's property?"

"I took a night hike with Rick," Nikki said. "Looked around a little. That's all."

"And Gunner found the burial grounds? And then Rick sent in the so-called birdwatchers—" Sonja paused to make air quotes with her fingers— "who reported their find to the game warden?"

"Something like that." Nikki lowered her voice. "But Justin can't know. He likes everything by the book."

"I'm sure he bends the rules on occasion," Sonja said, "when the end justifies the means. That new commissioner certainly doesn't seem able to function without her right- hand man. But don't worry, your secret is safe with me."

They both glanced at Justin who had moved on from Gunner and was now rubbing the pony's neck. Stormy had his head stretched out, eyes rolling in bliss. Justin always knew the right spots to touch. No wonder animals loved him. And women too.

He glanced up, as if sensing her gaze, and his slow wink made her wonder if he could hear their conversation. But there was no way he knew she'd sneaked onto Durant's property.

He would have been appalled, not only because of the danger but also because of the legalities. That was exactly the reason she'd chosen private work over law enforcement. Following police procedures was way too limiting.

No, she reassured herself. He had no idea what she and Rick had done. She'd glossed over her encounter with Durant and his men, blamed her restlessness on residual horrors from the pig case. But hopefully the "random" bone discovery would drag Durant down. At least local police were no longer in charge. The FBI had inexplicably taken over although she didn't know the details. Could only hope for justice.

She stretched her legs out on the new foot stool, trying to stay in the moment. Thoughts of Durant beating potential charges only darkened an otherwise perfect outcome for Ana and Jorge. They even had made enough money for Jorge's sister to join them in Chile, far from Durant's reach. Chico had paid his loyal backers well.

"I see you bought furniture to go with the new veranda," Nikki said. "How much did you win on Chico's race?"

"Almost as much as Ana. I also picked the horses that came third and fourth."

Nikki's eyes widened. The exactor bets she'd laid on Ana's behalf had paid out more than enough to cover airfare. But if Sonja had picked the top four horses, she would have had a much bigger return. Hitting the superfecta was difficult, especially with two longshots. Even Justin rarely managed it.

"That's fantastic you were so lucky."

"Lucky?" Sonja raised an elegant eyebrow. "You do know I'm a psychic?"

"But you said it was hard to connect with horses, especially from a distance."

"Hard but not impossible. And Chico is smart. It was his sense of the competition that made the difference."

"Too bad he's now in South America. At least you had one lucrative race."

"Not just one race. I've laid some bets since. It's way more fun than reading tea leaves."

Nikki shifted, crossing and uncrossing her legs. Sonja relied on earnings from her psychic business and sometimes struggled to pay rent. The bulk of her money was devoted to animal rescue. And while sports betting might be more exciting, it was also risky.

"Justin says betting should be for entertainment," Nikki said, picking her words carefully. "That people shouldn't expect to make money."

"It was Justin who set me up with my new betting program."

Nikki straightened so fast her feet thumped the floor. It didn't make sense that Justin would encourage Sonja. He was even more skeptical than her about a psychic's ability.

Sonja rose to her feet with a jaunty grin. "Like I said, he knows the score. That's why he's always one step ahead of everyone. And once I get to know his horses, this betting is going to get even more interesting.

"I'll make more coffee," she added, pulling open the screen door and stepping inside.

Nikki rubbed her forehead, her gaze turning to Justin. He'd finished with Gunner and Stormy—much to their chagrin—and was reading a message on his phone.

Pivoting, he climbed the steps, all traces of the playful animal-loving man gone.

"Do you need to go back to work?" she asked, studying his somber expression.

"Not until tomorrow." He held out his phone. "This is about a different matter."

She wordlessly took his cell. Justin didn't talk about his cases, always kept things compartmentalized. And this was his work phone so it was odd he was handing it over.

The text on his screen was brief: *Confirmed remains of Gloria Cortes. Two additional male bodies awaiting ID. Durant to be arrested today. As requested, world race media will be tipped.*

She pressed the phone against her chest, relief warring with dismay. She'd always feared Gloria had been murdered. She'd also been afraid Durant might never have his day in court so this news was bittersweet.

"They got him?" she said. "They really got him?"

"Yes. Once the FBI took over, things moved quickly. Apparently Durant's DNA is all over the female victim."

"I can't believe it. He's really going to face charges?"

"Absolutely," Justin said. "But it's lucky those birdwatchers got lost and stumbled over the burial site. Otherwise a search warrant would never have been granted. Even if it was, Durant's property is so vast that sniffer dogs would have had a tough time. Unless, of course, it was an exceptional dog."

"Very exceptional," she murmured, handing back his phone, careful not to look at Gunner. Careful also not to admit that Rick had extracted valuable information from Durant, in those few minutes when he'd been alone with the man behind the track chute.

"I'm surprised you're following the case," she added. "You have so many of your own."

"I found it interesting, especially considering your friendship with Ana. I actually called Rick Talbot at the Riverview track to see what he could tell me about Durant."

She folded her arms, suddenly feeling vulnerable. She wasn't ready to talk about the assault. Or admit that she'd sneaked onto Durant's property. She didn't know which event would worry Justin most—her rashness at chasing an intruder over a fence or how she and Rick had trespassed in order to dig up evidence. He was also unlikely to refer her agency for any more police work if he thought she'd resort to illegal means.

"Talbot didn't talk details," Justin went on. "Only said that Durant had the local police in his pocket. So I thought it would help if I pushed the FBI to get involved."

"I'm glad you did." She swallowed, annoyed at the crack in her voice. "Because he hurt everyone around him. Ana and the other victims will be relieved he'll finally pay."

"He absolutely will pay." Justin spoke with such ferocity, she glanced up, scanning his face.

"I'm surprised you didn't question me," she said. "Before calling the FBI. You're usually so meticulous."

"You didn't want to talk about it. And I knew enough. Even if the bones turned out to be animal, the scandal would destroy

Durant's reputation, something that he values. He resents his father's success and wants to beat him at everything."

Justin's knowledge was impressive. She hadn't told him much about Durant, or the bones, or her suspicions. Had never imagined he'd go after someone without concrete evidence. Would never have asked that.

"I may have been affected by what Talbot told me," Justin added. "That Durant was especially brutal with horses. And women. And anyone who dared to help his staff."

She rubbed her arms. Thinking about that night—how she'd fallen for Durant's trap—still raised a chill. She didn't want to admit she'd made such a rookie mistake.

"Whatever Rick Talbot told you," she said, "is probably exaggerated."

"He said you and Gunner showed remarkable restraint when you collared Durant. And how much your dog trusts you. Is that an exaggeration?"

"Not exactly," she said, swept with a warm glow. "Did he say anything else?"

"Just more praise about your dog. Clearly we're lucky to have Gunner on our approved K9 list. Although I'm not sure why he thinks Gunner has such a good nose...since, you know, Rick Talbot only saw him at the track."

"Yes, that's odd."

She peered up, trying to figure out how much Justin knew. But he'd mastered the deadeye cop stare and he wasn't giving anything away. Then she caught the twitch of his lip, the amusement leaking from the corners of his mouth.

"How did you know?" she asked, smiling back at him.

"You've been talking in your sleep," he said, kneeling down and entwining his fingers in hers. "So I decided to nail that creep. But there was one Tuesday morning that you and Gunner were both oddly exhausted. I checked the pads of his feet. They were worn, some cuts too. I should have guessed you already had something in motion. The only thing left for me to do was pull some strings with the Bureau."

"It's not like you to take something so personally."

"It is when it involves you."

She stared into his dark eyes, moved by his rare show of emotion. This man loved her. She just had to learn to believe it.

"When you're ready," he went on, "let's talk about what happened. I know you want to make your own way but I like to hear about your exploits. No matter what I've got going on."

"Okay." She swallowed back the lump in her throat. "But it might be awhile before I land a case as exciting as the last two. My stuff isn't like yours. Most of my jobs are boring."

His smile turned wry. "If only that were true."

OTHER BOOKS BY BEV PETTERSEN

About The Author

USA *Today* Bestselling Author Bev Pettersen is a three-time nominee in the National Readers Choice Award as well as the winner of many other international awards including the Reader Views Reviewer's Choice Award, Aspen Gold Reader's Choice Award, Write Touch Readers' Award, Kirkus Recommended Read, and a HOLT Medallion Award of Merit. She competed on the Alberta Thoroughbred race circuit and is an Equestrian Canada certified coach.

Bev lives in Nova Scotia with her family—humans and four-legged—and when she's not writing novels, she's riding. If you'd like to know about special offers or when her next book will be available, please visit her at http://www.BevPettersen.com where you can sign up for a newsletter.

Made in the USA
Las Vegas, NV
11 September 2024

95161059R00111